Bad Habit

Bad Habit

Alana S. Portero

Translated from the Spanish by Mara Faye Lethem

4th ESTATE • *London*

4th Estate
An imprint of HarperCollins*Publishers*
1 London Bridge Street
London SE1 9GF

www.4thestate.co.uk

HarperCollins*Publishers*
Macken House, 39/40 Mayor Street Upper,
Dublin 1, D01 C9W8, Ireland

First published in Great Britain in 2024 by 4th Estate
First published in the US in 2024 by HarperVia
Originally published as *La mala costumbre* in Spain in 2023 by Seix Barral

1

A catalogue record for this book is
available from the British Library

ISBN 978-0-00-866329-2 (Hardback)
ISBN 978-0-00-866330-8 (Trade paperback)

MIX
Paper | Supporting
responsible forestry
FSC™ C007454

This book contains FSC™ certified paper and other controlled
sources to ensure responsible forest management.

For more information visit: www.harpercollins.co.uk/green

For Maria Cardona, who is τύχη

I remember when living was dangerous, but we felt
alive.
I remember when taking hormones was suicide.
I remember when lipsticks and semen tasted of
cotton candy.
I remember when we were a fire flaming out of control.
I remember when we were happy. I remember when we
could be heroes.
I remember when we turned into sheep to be flesh
for the hunters.
I remember when I didn't want to die. Technically I'm
already dead.

ROBERTA MARRERO

CONTENTS

Bad
Habit

THE FALLEN ANGEL

saw a whole generation of boys fall like irredeemable angels. Teenagers with gray skin and missing teeth, reeking of ammonia and urine. Their foreshortened figures flanked the exit to the San Blas metro station on Calle Amposta and the small meadows of Parque El Paraíso, like Mantegna's Christs. Covered in needles like Saint Sebastian. Sitting or sprawled out any which way. Barely moving, slow and syncopated like broken dolls. With the sublime smile of the crucified. Defenseless but already floating in places where nothing could touch them. I saw them sprout and slacken before finally reaching stillness and decomposing in the mud that collected in our neighborhood that, despite its holy namesake, remained utterly godforsaken.

The first time I fell in love it was with one of those angels. He came flying from the window of his parents' apartment, which was right above our 375-square-foot ground-floor place, a hypodermic needle planted in his foot. My neighbor Efrén. He wound up dead on the street, half naked, in front of my door. I wasn't yet six years old, I wore a patch on one eye, and I stuttered. I think it was his mother's wailing that alerted the other inhabitants of our building, three floors with no entryway, just stairs on the outside. We got there before the police, who took their time responding to any call from our neighborhood, San Blas. To them, to every authority, he was just another dead junkie, the son of some woman dog-tired from mopping stairwells, the apple of her eye who'd probably already ransacked her home numerous times to shoot up more smack.

The truth is, I don't remember Efrén alive. I only have the image I was able to steal from between the legs of my mother and my neighbor Lola with the only eye I had, as if peering through a peephole. The mothers in my neighborhood didn't embrace their dead children like the virgins in Renaissance pietàs did. Instead, they hunched over their bodies, screaming, hair wild, eyes swollen, drooling. Shielding their babies best they could, covering them like desperate beasts, calling out to them until they lost their voice there on the sidewalk, as their nails gouged their flesh, departing with them somehow.

Those cries of "No, not my boy!"—if you've heard them—never leave you. They remain in the sound files of your memory like death knells, forcing you to shake your head to exorcise them.

Efrén was gorgeous, and the abyss was kind to his gentle features that had yet to reach manhood. An overdose carried him off to the other side. He hadn't been hooked long, and heroin had scarcely begun to mold his face, just tinged his skin ashen. It was the first time I wanted to kiss anyone. His body was sprawled before a scrawny garden that grew in front of our building, right below one of the entrance arches badly covered by half-dry flowers and ivy veins that barely enshrouded the crude wire structure. In spite of it all, death had chosen a botanical frame with a certain gritty art nouveau flair for Efrén. His mouth was slightly agape and his lips fleshy, not yet withdrawn; his hair was messy and his eyelids somewhere between wakefulness and sleep. If it's possible for a five-year-old to fall in love, then my love poured completely onto that tragic wreck. My inner life unfurled over that still frame of pain and misery, projecting myself floating, translucent above that corpse, kissing him with the lightness of beings that do not exist, not trying to wake him from his lethargy, not so he would kiss me back. I simply yearned with my entire soul to kiss something so lovely and helpless. Something that seemed fallen from heaven, left like an ex-voto on my doorstep. Something that, amid the sound and fury of drooling mothers and fathers who covered their mouths to repress their sobs, I somehow understood belonged to me.

THE WITCH AT THE
END OF MY STREET

The Wig was super short, thin as a rake, and wrinkled in such a way that as she stirred, she seemed to be interrupting some inexorable mummification. She was always old. She was made up like a caricature of an old lady, with blue eyeshadow, black liner, red lips, and a perfectly cracked foundation of Mona-Lisa-potato-colored skin. She smelled like dead flowers forgotten in a drawer and constantly whispered a string of unintelligible words under her breath, like a secret prayer laced with poison. The poison had to do with her surly, mocking gaze. Her seriousness wasn't the judgmental kind, but rather, the type that presaged a hearty laugh, as if every time she looked at someone, an embarrassing secret about them was revealed to her.

She lived alone at the end of the street, a row of three-story redbrick apartment buildings with concrete stairs at the front. That architectural motif repeated throughout the entire neighborhood, occasionally interrupted by some battered lot flush with broken glass, scraps of aluminum foil, needles, and abandoned building materials. If we could've spied the pavement from above, those gaps in the rows of apartment buildings must have made it look like diseased gums where enormous teeth had been yanked out with no apparent logic, leaving behind an incurable infection and lumpy holes. Besides the park and the housing itself, the rest was dumping grounds, empty lots where the neighborhood kids played and—when they were old enough to shoot up—where they went to die. We grew up like that: generations of working-class kids dreaming up whole worlds in the very same plots that one day might become our final resting places.

The garden didn't reach The Wig's corner. The view from her ground-floor apartment (if she'd ever pulled up the green blinds that covered her window day and night) was of garbage cans.

Our buildings were part of a large Francoist housing development built in the fifties, dubbed the Great San Blas. The former name, Cow Ridge, must've stunk of sweat and shit to the fascist authorities. Meanwhile, the debt collectors who combed door-to-door referred to it as "the motherless neighborhood" because they were usually greeted by children who should've been at school. It hadn't occurred to the visionaries of the regime that more than thirty thousand families would expect schools nearby for their kids, and it was years before that need was met. Along with the need for running water and for shops. Workers were never treated by Franco's regime as anything more than pack mules—to be herded into the city's outskirts. This generated a class consciousness in the neighborhood that later authorities—during the transition to democracy following Franco's death—conspired to weed out with jabs of heroin so cheap, they were practically free. In the late seventies and eighties, drugs were the last manifestation of summary executions for dissidents, employed by an old regime that had found a way to survive.

There were four things the neighborhood said about The Wig: that she'd worked in the black market up in the mountain caves; that she was quite a competent witch; that casting spells had left her bald; and that it was best to avoid her or, failing that, to treat her with extreme caution if you had no choice but to share a landing or the line at the produce market with her. It was hard to not gawk at the very curly, exceedingly shoddy synthetic hairpiece that graced her head. But you had to find a way. The Wig was not just her nickname, it was also a trigger for her maliciousness, and it was not in your best interests to provoke her.

It drove me wild to run into her and deeply inhale her scent;

it was like snorting moths. I knew I was supposed to fear her, but I was moved by her appearance, her irregular, trembling strokes of eyeliner, her sloppy lipstick application. It reminded me of my own clandestine makeup sessions, the cosmetics hastily applied in my grandmother's bathroom by the hand of a five-year-old not particularly gifted with a brush.

My baby steps into cross-dressing were a four-foot quick-change artist's imitation of an old witch who peddled secondhand goods and smelled like a funeral home.

The men in my neighborhood truly feared her. Rugged factory laborers, construction workers, waiters, vendors, scrap collectors, folks who did what they could to get by—all alike would lower their gaze and mumble "Good afternoon" to her like kids addressing a priest in the years following the civil war. It was comical, actually, to see them with their chests peeking out of half-buttoned shirts, passing her on their way to the bar after back-breaking workdays, intimidated by a woman who seemed so fragile.

Hardly anyone could even remember her real name. And while everyone knew her nickname, it was never spoken in her presence, not just because it was cruel and spiteful but mostly out of a fear of her reaction. Everyone addressed her as "ma'am."

Once, two women who lived on the same street as The Wig, both of them pregnant, went for a walk to relieve the swelling that comes with carrying a child during a particularly sweltering summer. One of them had suffered circulation problems in her legs since she was a girl, and had to walk to alleviate the swelling of the purple floaties on her ankles. The two young women had made a habit of strolling together in the evenings, chatting about the news and routines of their pregnancies, fears, dreams, and the latest gossip. In a neighborhood where everybody knew everybody else, there was always some rumor or other, and an eager audience for scuttlebutt.

The woman with the purply legs usually harped on about her dream of a matador son who would buy her a big house "like the radio said El Cordobés bought for his mother." The other, slightly younger, envisioned a very handsome son, "kinda blond, with light eyes," she would say.

They had just started out on their walk when they saw The Wig approaching from the far end of the street and, exploiting the distance, quickly heaped on their lazy, cruel jokes about the old woman's looks.

"Stop, stop, I'm gonna piss my pants," pleaded the one with the swollen feet to her younger counterpart, who employed a quick imagination and a viper's tongue. They were both young, in their early twenties, and reveling in all the cruelty youth is capable of. Which is a lot. Regrets and restraint come with decrepitude, as does selfishness, when suddenly we find ourselves on the flip side of life and acknowledge that there's hardly an ugly thing that won't eventually find us.

They managed to stifle their laughter and brutal razzing long before crossing paths with The Wig. When nearly by her side, both began to smile deferentially in anticipation, the proper attitude afforded an older neighbor. But they didn't have a chance. The Wig stopped short in front of them, her little body a dead bush that seemed to take up the entire sidewalk. The pregnant women tried to say good afternoon, but the words caught in their throats like acid reflux. Most likely, their instinct was to bring their hands to their bellies. The old lady's gaze—present and absent at the same time—radiated something that could wither everything in its path, be it flowers, joys, or placentas. Then The Wig leisurely lifted her left hand up to the pasty hole she had for a mouth and stuck in her thumb, sucking on it with gusto, swabbing it around, savoring it with loud slurps, all while keeping her eyes glued on the two women. For them, time had stopped. They embodied a low-frequency but paralyzing fear underscored by a vast discomfort and helplessness. Once The Wig had her thumb well lathered in saliva, she calmly brought it straight from her mouth to the cheek of one of the pregnant women. The one with the viper's tongue. The one who dreamed of a handsome, gorgeous son. Kinda blond, with light eyes.

She couldn't dodge the thumb; she had no time to react. The old lady traced a straight line of spittle from the cheekbone to nearly the chin of that young face plump with pregnancy, declaring loudly, and with a lizard's voice: "Monkey."

I barely knew Damián. He and his mother rarely left the house, and when they did, he was always covered up and obscured by a stroller hood. People said he couldn't walk and suffered a skin affliction that made exposure to the sun lethal. He didn't speak. He died of a stroke at the age of six, lying on a couch at home, watching television. When they arrived to pick up his corpse, his mother placed a handkerchief over his little hairy face so they wouldn't tease him on his way to the morgue.

My mother's circulatory problems cleared up, and instead of a matador, she gave birth to a trans daughter who still has yet to buy her a big house.

SAY MY NAME

You discover that you'll end up becoming a woman from the examples that surround you; from your thirst for role models; from your need to take part in the legacy, the inheritance some women bequeath to others, of which men know nothing.

It was a bad idea to press your luck with The Wig. That tiny lady exuded power from every one of her stretched seams. Of course, I spoke to her as soon as I got the chance. It's not that I expected to acquire the ability to ruin pregnancies or other terrible powers. Or maybe I did. But I understood that there was something encircling her, something that caused her to be rejected, and it made me very sad. I pictured her doing her makeup each morning with the clumsiness of someone whose nervous system is no longer entirely her own, someone who already has ceded a part of her anatomy and abilities to the darkness to come. Even still, she never missed an appointment with that mask, just as I never missed the construction of mine every morning. The difference was that hers, at some point, must have exuded power and beauty, even though now it was in shambles. If we had known how to look, surely the shadow of her splendor was still there, but the ability to see it eluded us. My mask was one to hide behind, a mask of shame and fear, something I shouldn't have needed, or even known existed, at that age.

That was why I had to speak to her, because there was some inheritance, however meager, that I needed from her, so I could continue constructing the woman I would become.

I was a clever girl, a closeted queer, a stutterer, chubby, with a patch covering my left eye and oversized glasses. The aura I gave off was the antithesis of an unruly, disobedient child, and I didn't seem to harbor the innocent cruelty of most children. When adults looked me up and down, they either felt amused or a slight twinge of pity. I reminded them how athletic and poised their own children were; that reassured them. My presence was calming to grown-ups, except for those truly mean ones. I realized that and learned to use it to my advantage. I was capable of thinking in ruthless terms. The awareness that you need a closet to hide in makes you a very adept player of the game of truth and lies, shrewd about what you reveal and what you conceal.

I waited to stage a chance encounter, doodling on the lower stairs with a piece of brick. The Wig passed my house at least four times a day on her mysterious walks, lugging very full plastic bags.

"I know the names of all the ladies on this street."

I delivered it in the voice of a little girl imitating an even smaller girl, because you also learn how to be a bona fide devious daughter of a bitch when you apply makeup in secret and dance to Raffaella Carrà and Bonnie Tyler songs in your room, knowing it all points to the fact that you are destined for a complicated life.

"Oh, really?" the old woman responded, choking on the dryness of her own throat, so unaccustomed to speaking aloud except for curses.

"Yes. Señora Lola, Señora Paca, Señora Luisa, Señora Amparo, Señora Mercedes, Señora Pascuala . . ."

That was how the list sounded in my head, but in reality, I had tripped on the first "Señora," since every "S" is a wart on a stutterer's tongue.

"Speak properly!" she scolded, no longer choking. With just two words, she'd warmed up that esparto grass throat of hers. She declared it sternly but not cruelly. Like giving an order. And it worked. I chanted the list of ladies on my street like a Hail Mary and was tempted to continue, to list the entire catalogue of martyrs, if I'd known it, just to hear myself speak without a stutter.

"And what about me? Don't I live on this street?" More than irate, she seemed amused by her own interjection.

That was when I, starry-eyed, sprung the subtle trap I had

set. With the gestures of a wounded fawn, a dose of smugness, and dead-easy lure, I was going to find out her name. Knowing a witch's name isn't like learning a demon's; you can't wield it to control them or invoke them, but you can address them familiarly, and it's never a bad idea to have a witch in your back pocket. It was in my best interest to use this occasion to earn The Wig's trust by knowing how to address her properly.

I was expecting her to have a mysterious name, like an ancient Roman or fairy-tale sorceress, Grimelda, Morgana, Salustia, I don't know, some word with three syllables that involved guttural, dental sounds that crunch inside your mouth.

"My name is María."

At least it had three syllables.

"My name is Aaaa . . . Aaa . . ."

Open vowels are closed valves in stutterers' throats. Her spell had worn off.

"I know your name. I've known your mother since she was a little girl. And your father since he sold sweet buñuelos in the park on a tray bigger than him. And your grandparents. Didn't they ever tell you my name?"

She prodded with surgical transparency; there was no mistaking it. She had moved her dialectical bishop to the very same square where my discursive king sat. She was the one who had set a trap for me. I had to make up a lie or an excuse quickly before I pissed my pants in shame.

But, whatever the reason, it seemed that, when I'd gotten up that morning, I'd chosen the path of violence. I was surprised to hear myself expose a truth not even the shadiest guys in the neighborhood dared say in front of that woman. There should be no lies between us, so I just blurted it out.

"The Wig. They always call you The Wig." If she was going to carpet my guts in ivy with some fast-acting evil eye, I preferred to go down in a blaze of pluck and personality.

She looked at me from that paralysis of dead tissue encasing her. Simultaneously present and absent. Like the gaze of a mounted head on a hunter's wall. With the animosity and glassy patience of someone waiting on the other side of life's veil and who, despite her weakness on this plane, holds sway in the great beyond, her spectral existence dominating almost entirely.

"Ah, The Wig," she said from that great distance.

If that wasn't the beginning of the slowest roar of laughter in the history of the world, at least it seemed eternal to me. It was like watching the bark on a particularly rough pine tree change attitude. I ended up joining in. We passed the contagious laughter back and forth for a good long while, until someone paused for a moment to contemplate the scene. A little kid scarcely more than a baby (and not very pretty) and a grotesque old woman who were having a ball, for some reason only the two of them understood. In that moment, Doña María didn't seem sinister to me, not in the slightest. When we laugh wholeheartedly, we inhabit no age. We do it in exactly the same way throughout our lives, and in our cackling expressions, you can glimpse both the little girls we once were and the old ladies we will become.

In that inconsequential instant, very few things separated us. I hadn't been mistaken in my choice of role model, even if this was the end and we never spoke again. Women who live the way they want, who age on their own terms and wear their lives etched into their faces, are treated with pathos and mockery because they are feared.

"Go on now, hurry inside, it's getting late. And tell your parents to take that thing off your eye."

"It's lazy and it wanders."

"It's your left eye; that eye is never wrong. If it looks in a different direction from the other, heed it. It's telling you to see something."

I thought about informing her that it was just a slight malformation of the ocular nerve that was easily corrected. I loved medical jargon and was very curious, so I had carefully memorized what was going on with my eye to explain it whenever I got the chance. The way I memorized everything. I decided I shouldn't overwhelm Señora María after the laugh we'd shared. If I hoped to become a grande dame, I had to know when to let things go. After all, she'd just spared my life and been kind enough to cast a spell so I could speak a few phrases without stumbling. So all I said was: "You smell really good, Señora María."

"Don't lay it on too thick."

Her words cracked like a whip, and she was already walking off, her back to me, resuming her pilgrimage to the park. As if our moment of complicity had never happened. I saw her soon disappear, moving quickly despite being weighed down by plastic bags full of God-knows-what. Surely not bread crumbs. I couldn't imagine her feeding the birds. More likely she was burying their crunchy carcasses beneath the black poplars on Avenida de Arcentales or under the pines in Parque El Paraíso.

BLUEBEARD
LIVES ON THE
GROUND-FLOOR LEFT

"ÉH TÉH TÉH TÉH TÉH TÉH ..."

"That poor Gema, what a day she's been having. She's driving me nuts. Loud téh-téh-téhs since four in the morning. Your father got up an hour earlier because there was no way to keep sleeping. That poor girl, it's agony, such a shame ..."

My mother was brewing coffee in the kitchen, so cramped only she could fit inside, while also stripping green beans and peeling potatoes. I watched her from a chair in the living room, my feet dangling.

Gema was a daughter of our neighbors directly across the hall. Each floor in our building housed two units, starting with the ground floor, whose doors, including ours and theirs, opened onto the street. On the upper floors they opened onto an exterior landing for the stairs. I had only ever spied Gema through a tiny little window that overlooked the backlot, a concrete expanse covered in garbage, rats, and needles. Here some neighborhood boys occasionally played soccer, but it was mostly occupied by junkies, who had once played soccer there not long ago, to shoot up and sail away on the effects of the heroin, floating on that filthy surface like tar lily pads. That window was the only one Gema had in the room where her parents imprisoned her. She was older than twenty-five but she'd never seen anything more of the world than a tiny space opening onto nothing. Or at least, she'd ceased to belong to the world prematurely, as soon as her father, Aurelio, gauged that she would suit his repulsive, brutal sexual needs.

It was as simple as that. One day he made the decision to lock her up, and the world continued spinning as it always had. As an obsessive reader of stories, myths, and legends, I saw Gema—because of her loneliness, her long red hair, the silence enveloping her and her helplessness—as Lady Godiva. Ever since I could reason, and as a girl compelled to learn how to dwell in two realities because I had two lives, I would situate the women around me in fantasy spaces where nothing could touch them and where I would wander adrift, imagining stories woven in golden thread. I would see Aphrodites, Circes,

Nimues, and Elaines of Astolat at the 28 bus stop, on the platform of the Simancas metro station, or waiting in line at Señor Lucas's butcher shop. Sometimes I would stroke the hair of some of these strangers if they were in reach, sitting in front of my mother and me on public transport. I would twirl an errant lock around my index finger as if making a corkscrew curl, which seemed to me a laconic fairy-tale gesture, like Nereids combing each other's hair, and the women, when they realized, were often amused. My mother was always having to apologize for that habit of mine. Many nights I would fall asleep doing it to myself, just in case the path to becoming a nymph began with twirling your hair in the land of dreams.

I can't recall a single week when that miserable home didn't explode with Aurelio's wrath at least a few times. The only sounds that emerged from those walls were the sounds of screaming and hitting. No television, no radio, no conversations. Nothing except Lady Godiva's convulsive "téh téh téh."

Aurelio came and left with no fixed routine. He had no known job, although folks suspected he was mixed up in the petty dealing of the drugs killing off the sons and daughters of his neighbors. He usually initiated his aggressions upon returning from his wanderings—any excuse sufficed: something out of place, a sideways glance, or a simple "Is that you?" innocently asked in greeting.

"Yes, it's me, it's me. *What are you*, blind?"

He always responded like that, lashing out with a sarcastic question.

"Well, I wasn't expecting you so soon," his wife, Luisa, would say, trying to calm what was brewing.

"Wasn't expecting you sooOOon," the tyrant would interrupt, raising his pitch into the derisive voice men use to imitate women, screwing up his face as he mocked her.

It didn't take much more. Aurelio was methodical and consistent in carrying out his abuse. He wasn't one to flare up briefly. There was a meticulous, poisoned discipline to his brutality. He would goad with uncomfortable or vague questions, taunting whoever tried to answer them, insisting, asking again, until finally he began to unleash his blows in exercised restraint. You could hear the walls quake, furniture shuffling, footsteps drawn out, even him directing his victim—his wife or one of his three children—to position themselves in such a way that he could lay into them more easily. It was unbearable, and if extreme violence ever managed to inhabit a comfortable routine, it was in that home. It happened the way mundane things happen, obscuring the fact that they are perfectly avoidable.

The son of a bitch began his liturgy again on that morning of coffee and green beans and potatoes. Every time he started in on his family while I was at home, I would be deathly afraid. I'd always ask my mother to turn up the radio or to sing loudly, as she often did. The poor woman would usually anticipate the situation; she knew how to read the signs. When the radio volume was up too loud for no reason or Mamá was singing her lungs out, some song by Nicola Di Bari, Adamo, or Marifé de Triana, it meant the devil was dancing in the apartment across the way.

I locked myself in the room I shared with my brother, which luckily had no windows and was not adjacent to any other apartment. Yet a vibration in the walls was impossible to ignore, and I thought about Laura, the family's youngest daughter, my Joan of Arc, with her short bob with straight bangs and her willingness to battle even hell itself. She usually had to swallow a very bitter slice of the poison pie her father dished out. She was sixteen years old, and everything about her screamed rebellion. Her feline green eyes, her grave expression, her hoarse voice, and her aesthetic—more goth than punk, but edging more extreme with each passing day since she knew her style turned her father's stomach. I loved her so much. Laura would paint my nails in secret, and I would clean them before anyone saw. She would also do the nails of another sissy boy in the neighborhood, uglier and far more in need of such attention than me, the son of a mechanic whom my father had known forever.

I knew that Laura's attitude cost her, that her abuser laid into her with particular enmity—you didn't need to be a grown-up to understand that—but often I couldn't help begging her to be good in case that would help to mitigate the brutality. That sexist violence is meted out independently of what we women do or don't do was something I had yet to learn.

The whole neighborhood knew what Laura did for a living since quitting school as soon as it was legal to do so. It was spoken of in hushed tones or euphemistically, as if that softened the abnormality of a teenager working the industrial areas, parks, or streets downtown, fucking guys in search of an underage fantasy at a good price. As broken as she was—much more by her father's slimy hand than by those losers paying for a minor's attention—she remained strong and never bowed her head. She was repulsed by the pity she received everywhere she went around the neighborhood, their lack of tact when trying to convey empathy. They didn't know how to show it any better, and she understood that too, although that didn't lessen her scorn. Soon after that, I stopped seeing her. When she cobbled together enough money, she finally escaped the ground-floor left apartment, becoming a recurring thought for me, a prayer of hope, a triumphant myth, a goddess of *if only*.

When the walls stopped trembling and the radio returned to its murmuring volume, I left my room. My mother had put more potatoes in the pot, and they'd cooked in the time it takes to deliver a beating. She mashed them with a fork, added oil, salt, and a dash of paprika, spread them out onto an amber glass plate before placing a clean dishcloth over them so they'd keep warm.

I knew what was coming now because it was always the same.

"I'll be right over." She said it the same way every time.

Then you could hear movement in the stairwell like in Mass, footsteps so discreet, they seemed hesitant to trouble the floor.

Aurelio's sadistic method was perfectly predictable. Once the brutish hour was over, he went out for some fresh air, as if he'd earned it. He was usually slow to come back. In that lapse of time, the neighbor ladies, almost all of them, approached Luisa's house with something to eat, some clothes, or a hot drip coffee. They had no other way to show their support. They'd stopped calling the police because all they ever did was take Aurelio out of the house, talk to him until he seemed calm, and dismiss him with a ridiculous warning and Sunday school advice. It wasn't unusual that the jerk would wait only a few minutes after the police left before resuming his torture at the same juncture where it had been interrupted.

When the neighborhood women brought over dishes, containers, and jars, they always added a "How you doing?" What else could you say or do when there was no support structure to help that woman? Mamá returned with her eyes brimming with tears, and she smiled at me with a grimace laden with pity.

"Come on, help me trim the ends of these beans. Carefully. Hold the knife firmly and do it like this. . . . That's it. Good job. Now do the same thing with the whole pile."

I held on to memories like that, to treasure forever. I was afraid my parents would stop loving me if they knew I wasn't who they thought I was. Listening to grown-ups speak of people who were different left marks that never went away. We girls are always listening, and you never know if what is budding within each of us might be permanently crippled by a single word. I also knew that what they could see of me, they adored, and that of course, neither of them would ever be like Aurelio.

I wondered why the men didn't intervene. In my childhood world, they were the ones who fought monsters and kept the peace. In other circumstances, they confronted each other without hesitation, without real cause. I saw a lot of the men in my neighborhood come to blows over a parking space, some absurd misunderstanding, or a dirty look. Things they used more to dispute the pecking order than to establish any sort of justice.

My father often talked to us about the problems workers faced, about sticking together, about fighting the good fight so that everyone had the basics covered and some respect. At daybreak on the morning of the first general strike after Franco's death, ducking our mother's reasonable opposition, he stole us out of bed to go with him and his union brothers to seal the doors of our neighborhood's warehouses and plants with silicone. Afterwards, taking the logical precautions, he shepherded us to the picket line to bulk up the numbers and so we'd learn, firsthand, what it was like. My brother and I were too young to understand it. For us it was a chance to spend time with our father, whom we didn't see much because of his endless workdays, and a chance to play at something strange and really fun together. When the morning came and some scabs tried to push past the picketers, there followed the usual pandemonium of shoving and insults. My father made sure that we witnessed everything that was going on, that it was seared into our young minds, trusting that, over time, we would learn how to interpret that rage in all its complexity. It wasn't a happy ending to our adventure—we were in fact quite scared—but it was useful.

In any case, that was how my father did things: his way of showing love was to never lie to us, to nudge our maturity along, and to show a respect for our judgment rarely afforded to children. The first thing I understood was that a scab, a word I often heard and found very intriguing, was someone who turned on his own and betrayed them to get ahead or, even worse, to maintain a lowly but more or less secure position. Maybe scab-shaming didn't apply to the domestic sphere. Maybe betraying women was incomparable to outing yourself as a *worm* in front of your brothers on the union team, another sacred word. Whatever the reason, it was clear that the men in our building didn't think it was appropriate to intervene in a situation like that of the tyrant in the ground-floor left apartment.

They did give Aurelio the cold shoulder: no one talked to him or included him in the Sunday beers. But the men in the apartment building passed the buck, arguing that they didn't like other people sniffing around in their houses and that marriage problems were a couple's private business. Calling that monstrous abuse a "problem" was a significant exercise in cynicism; they never would have used such language around labor conflicts. It was strange. They all knew he was a jerk. They said he was a criminal. They were disgusted by him, but it seemed that every man had a picket line around him, one no one dared cross.

FLOATING OVER THE DEBRIS

Saúl, Aurelio and Luisa's middle child, dressed like Tino Casal, spoke like I imagined Momo's friend Gigi Cicerone would, and strutted like Pete Burns. I loved watching him waltz in and out of his house, seeing him walk towards the metro station until he vanished around the corner, clicking his heels joyfully. He was gorgeous, with the same malicious green eyes as his sister Laura. The blemishes on his face left by his father's fists were perfectly visible and his collection of scars kept growing, but despite that, he seemed determined to carry on with his life and disappear from there soon. Which is what he ended up doing.

Sometimes I wanted to be like him. Fascinating, unique, and feminine. They would call him a faggot, make fun of him, and threaten him daily. They never let up on him in our neighborhood, so he rarely set foot there except to sleep, and as he got older, not even that. He somehow managed to walk above the dumpsite that he'd been dealt as a life, without breaking a sweat. He was Oberon: for his evil goblin eyes; for the gleam of his tunics; for his long, teased hair; for his ambiguous smile and his lips always painted in lovely colors. He had earned a spot in my legendarium of epic women, goddesses, grandes dames, and other exquisite creatures.

Except for the ghostly older sister, who never had a chance, Saúl and Laura were forged by the fires of another world. I was afraid of pretty much everything—incapable of living freely and happily, of being myself, without fear of losing the love, support, and security of my family. Yet in Saúl and Laura's immeasurable misfortune, they brewed up a cauldron of rage that spurred them on. I sensed that things were more complicated; I thought I could make out cracks in the armor of those creatures who were just beginning to live and had had the worst possible start, but I was fascinated by their strength. I never stopped thinking about them. I still haven't.

Saúl left without making any noise. He tousled my hair sweetly, still walking, one afternoon when I was watching the world in silence from the building's stairs. I think that was the last time I saw him. I don't remember him dragging any suitcases behind him, or even a backpack, nothing. I suppose the king of the fairies didn't need any baggage wherever he was headed.

SHINY GLIMMERS

had almost fallen asleep and drifted into the shadows of sentience, closer to the darkness than to wakefulness. I was resting on an immense leaf, perhaps a gigantic blade of grass, curved into a crescent hammock. I was naked and wet beneath the moonlight. I possessed no attributes—my body was pure phosphorescence with the consistency of plasma, of things half-baked—I was not yet flesh but already bore weight and a sense of touch. I was moving, but I wasn't—as my mind entered sleep, its ability to generate images slowed. I'd find a way to get flowing again once I fell deeper asleep. In that moment, our imaginations and what we understand as our unconscious, that lovely flow of chaotic thought, did what they could to maintain the visions. The sound—which was the sound of the night itself, a mix of crickets, wind, and spinning stars—muffled and almost vanished, or transformed into something else, something crystalline, something silvery, something that announced an end.

Right before the scream was heard, my skin bristled, and I opened my eyes wide. I was jolted back to reality like a package or a dead body dumped from a moving vehicle. A drop of sweat trickled from one end of my forehead to the other, never touching the pillow because it froze along with the rest of me. Another scream. And another shorter one. Many syncopated screams. Aurelio's voice was a howl, no trace of sadistic self-control, no hint of his butcher-like composure; it sounded like a piglet, hoarse dog, *fear*. I jumped out of bed, very frightened but determined to know what was going on. My brother, always super agile, had almost reached our small living room in a single leap from the upper bunk. My parents rushed out of their bedroom with the same urgency. My father had had time to pull on some sweatpants, and my mother was tying her robe as I reached them.

"Get into bed and lock the door, both of you! Jimena, call the police!" admonished my father. Not allowing any possible reply.

We didn't have time to complain because another horrific scream stifled our voices. My father opened the front door, which led directly onto the street, and strode out into the dawn. We heard other doors opening and heavy steps on the stairs, obviously men's; they reverberated like a stampede of heavy animals plunging from the heights of a cliff. The screams didn't stop and what little human quality they had diminished with each chorus. I thought I was going to faint from the panic. We hadn't gone back to our bedroom; disobeying my father, we remained paralyzed in the living room. My brother had positioned himself in front of me, protecting me as he always did. My mother spoke to the police, trembling. This time they wouldn't take so long to show up; they could probably hear Aurelio's desperate wails on the other side of the phone line and down the whole street.

What happened after that was a chaotic flux of bodies and voices. An ambulance arrived, or maybe two. There were so many flashing lights in front of our house that the night had been replaced by hysterically pulsating flickers. The walls were lit up: blue, white, red. I wanted to know what was going on, but I couldn't manage to move. The voices of the gathered crowd spliced into the radio transmissions from the squad cars and ambulances. My father came in and went back out; he looked at us but didn't see us. My mother, who had peeked outside a couple of times, brought her hands to her face and repeated, "Holy mother of God." As for my brother, he risked taking a few steps forward, enough to stand at the threshold of the door, left open in the chaos. I followed him and glanced over his shoulder. Lady Godiva was sitting on the floor of her house, perfectly visible because her door and ours were wide open, directly across from each other. The paramedics were attending to her. They spoke to her, but she didn't respond; she only smiled and gazed out towards places it seemed only she could access, and said, "Téh téh téh téh ..." in a loud voice but not shouting. If not for the blood pouring from her mouth, still fresh and staining her chin, neck, and the front of her nightgown, it would have been heartening to see her smile. It was the first time I'd ever seen that.

Aurelio was on the floor. A swarm of paramedics and police officers covered him like vultures polishing off the last carcass in the desert. When they'd finished with his urgent care, they lifted the stretcher and carried him off; the men carrying it had to swerve around the building's main staircase, a swerve which brought Aurelio's stretcher right in front of us for a moment. His head was cocked to one side, and we could glimpse his face. He was still complaining but now in a low moan; the painkillers they'd administered must have taken effect. He was so close to us that, if they hadn't been gouged out, his eyes surely would have stared back.

We went back to our bedroom as they took away Gema, who continued her litany of téh-téhs, almost singing it on her way to the ambulance. Lady Godiva had shed her skin and morphed into a Harpy.

THE GIRLS

I t smelled of chickpea stew with rice, and the sulfur from chopping onions still stung the air. The pressure cooker's valve spun quickly, letting out short bursts of steam that fogged up the kitchen windows. There were hardly any traces of prep, just a knife with hints of garlic and parsley in the sink. My mother proceeded quickly; she never resembled the mothers in books who donned floral aprons and handled all the ingredients with the patience of a weaver. She approached everything with the urgency of someone who had earned her living cleaning and cooking nonstop ever since she was old enough to know the wheels on the bus go round and round.

She wasn't careless or imprecise. In fact, she made delicious food from very little. She had simply developed a system informed by an obsession for getting things done, both at home and beyond it, a fixation that would never leave her. She wore an old T-shirt with a commercial logo and shorts. Something she could stain and toss into the wash as many times as needed. She was nimble and as spirited as a filly. She wore her hair short with highlights. She had a pretty, angular face with wide, heavy-lidded almond eyes and an imposing nose with a very prominent bridge that she could pull off with no problem. Her mouth was my best inheritance: proportioned with lips that were voluptuous without being too pronounced. She wasn't yet forty, but the skin on her face barely looked thirty. It was hard to believe that a woman who, since the age of twelve, had only known backbreaking work and poor nutrition could look so elegant. The signs of working-class rot would manifest some years later in her bones, but she would always have immaculate skin and a halo of impermeability to aging.

My mother always smelled like baby cologne and moisturizer. Despite smoking like she had a child in jail, she always seemed freshly showered. Like saints who defy putrefaction and still smell like flowers even in death.

She was very affectionate and didn't seem to hold a grudge against me for having forced her to give birth to a two-foot blockhead who weighed in at twelve pounds. We adored each other, and it would be our downfall. From a very young age, I understood that my mother dispensed a love that aspired to keep everything suspended in a perfect present where we remained immutable, or in which we carried out to a tee the life she'd imagined for us. Any detour along our projected path would always seem to her a defeat or leave an indelible mark of guilt on her heart. Ever since I'd been capable of structuring my thoughts, I'd wanted to tell her that I wasn't entirely me. That I was confused and that I was suffering, that my dancing to Irene Cara songs and obsession with Madonna had always been neon signs in the darkness and signified more than their apparent frivolity. They were jolts of freedom that I projected out onto the night sky, hoping—scared and expectant—that someone would be able to decipher them. The words never quite came out, and I didn't have the tools to undertake something so complicated that even I was anxious to bury it in a mass grave of shame.

I couldn't forget certain assertions that seemed so categorical and that I'd been hearing throughout my whole short life. As if my mother had caught some glimmer in me that she didn't like, and had hatched a subliminal plan to silence it. The fear you feel in the closet creates monsters out of shadow play. Every time she gushed about how happy she was to have two sons "even though Arturo really wanted girls, but I prefer boys; they're straight shooters, little lords." Or her insistence in calling us "tough guys" with extreme pride any chance she got, as if that moniker was a promise to be fulfilled as well as a reward bestowed on us for cleaning our plates or accomplishing some other task. They were small comments that gradually snowballed and seemed to describe another sort of creature who was not me. There was no malice in them, but my sensitive and conscientious nature registered them as warnings of the shame around any rejection of such roles. I wasn't *tough* or a straight shooter or any of those things, but little by little, I found myself trying to be, so that, in my mother's eyes, I wouldn't seem like the weak and disappointing opposite. Which was exactly what I wanted to be.

My mother buzzed quickly through the house to tidy it up. Fall was almost here, and the weather was very pleasant. One of those Saturday mornings in September when the energy of break still lingers as summer draws to a close, tempting us to ignore our obligations a little longer. That did not apply to the house chores as Mamá understood them. The house was like an extension of her own body, and she never let a day pass without cleaning it from top to bottom. A childhood filled with too many responsibilities had programmed her to never let herself down, under penalty of the wrath of the extolled lineage of strict mothers who believe no amount of scrubbing is ever enough.

We were a noisy family who lived in a noisy neighborhood. Peace and calm were for the rich districts. That morning, on the other side of the windows, you could hear the eternal buzz saw of crumbling working-class neighborhoods, where something always needed fixing. The lottery-ticket seller was doing his thing on the corner between two bars, singing out the number with the booming voice of a legionnaire. When he spun out on cheap wine, the bastard would sing the fascist "Cara al sol" at the top of his lungs, although he didn't usually get to the second line before some neighbor would tell him to can it, reminding the lottery seller that the only reason he wasn't busting his face was "cuz you're blind."

Over time, San Blas had grown into a hub of bars and small businesses, so there was a constant chorus of clinking glass and rolling beer kegs. There were always deliverymen dashing around, laden like mules. In our house, the radio would be on blast; that year, it was always playing Rick Astley, Whitney, Radio Futura, and U2 was king. Every once in a while, my mother changed the station, and then there'd be a Pantoja, a Jurado, some Panchos, and the occasional Camilo Sesto track. I can never thank my family enough for having such varied taste in music. At nine years old, I could sing with equal aplomb "Marinero de luces," "Little Wing," "Like a Virgin," or some sweet little bolero.

One morning, two of my mother's sisters were keeping her company as she worked. An older sister and a younger one. They shared an obvious family resemblance, but they hadn't all been equally blessed in the collagen department; my mother had hit the jackpot. They chatted over the music, which required a big effort but remained second nature. They were born extra: loud, excitable, and larger-than-life. They were very beautiful. I adored watching them, memorizing their gestures:

how they stood still, the way they would touch their hair, their blithe laughter, and how they handled objects. I absorbed the energy I could sense when women gathered together without men. I would dream about it; it gave me butterflies and a peace of mind I didn't find anywhere else. The time I spent with the men in my family left me cold inside and in constant tension. Boys didn't just grow up to be men; they were initiated into masculinity, and pity those who failed, even among the finest men. When I was in the company of the women in my family or my building, or the girls at my school, time slowed down as if it were bathed in hot water. I couldn't be one of them, I couldn't touch that life, but I could cherish what they taught me without even trying. It was like taking the most delicate and powerful myths off the pages of books and setting them walking so I could watch them. The path of the nymph, the witch, the White Queen, or the Harpy was beyond my reach, but there was something that allowed me to secretly weave that stowaway attention devoted to them into a tailor-made dress of femininity.

I was drawn to the magical gatherings of women in my family, but I maintained just enough distance to not make it obvious and not break the atmospheric spell with my ambiguous presence. I didn't always pull it off; they would often notice me and make a slightly annoyed remark about how I was always hanging around grown-ups, especially women. They figured I wanted to hear gossip, which I didn't contest because it was a good alibi. The bathroom was my private kingdom. There I would improvise quickly with makeup, improving my application each time, and I would practice what I'd learned by observing the women in my life. My sadness grew increasingly deep. The dysphoria, which I didn't even have a name for, took up so much mental space and created so much physical displeasure already at only nine friggin' years old, that there was hardly any room for anything else. At school, I was very capable, almost brilliant; in everything else, a disaster. I spent more time imagining than living, but I lacked the artistic talent to relieve my grief, I had no release valve, I didn't know how to paint my sad lot, I didn't dare write out of fear of leaving evidence. So I would dance and compartmentalize and fantasize scenes of my liberation. Above all, I would escape into literature, film, and music. I was a spectator to everything that surrounded me, unable to touch a thing.

I survived in public by adopting increasingly strict versions of the masculinity I had for an example, which was rampant. I practiced that too in front of the mirror, witness to all my lies, my pain, and my flashes of beauty. It was in front of the mirror that I learned to look at myself without seeing myself. To be an automaton.

"What are you doing in there, my boy?! You shit more than a pigeon! You can't keep locking yourself in there all the time.

One day something's gonna happen to you, and we'll have to bust the door down."

Direct, specific language with potent metaphors that pulled no punches—that was one of the characteristics that defined us as a family, and still does. We saw so much shit in the neighborhood, at work, and in life, there was no way we were going to call it by any other name. On the other hand, my mother's aversion to locks, especially when her sons were on the other side of the door, was over the top. She reacted so personally to a bolted door that you couldn't tell if she was very scared, very angry, or both. That was a bad match for a child in the closet. Behind that door, something important was usually going on. A parenthesis of liberation or a punishment session, but important either way. In the world of open doors, there was no room for swish or for sobs, only room for tough guys.

Years of clandestine practice had taught me to control the fleeting heart attack brought on by someone banging on the bathroom door while I was in the middle of some secret fairy shit. At first, when I was really little, when just holding a lipstick made me feel short of breath, someone knocking on the door felt like the devil himself was hammering his knuckles raw against the wood, demanding my poor little princess soul. Over time, I became capable of answering in the affected voice of a tough guy consumed by an urgent call of nature while I posed like Kelly LeBrock in front of the mirror.

"Your aunts and I are heading over to The Girls; you coming?"

No one could remember the actual name for The Girls—a very popular local clothing store—before it'd been rebaptized by the neighbors. It was an enormous place divided into two spaces: one for all the mandatory school uniforms and gym clothes, the other filled with countless racks and mannequins covered in women's clothing.

A fundamental part of my closeted façade consisted of feigning indifference towards things I was dying to do but which, if done with enthusiasm, would expose my not particularly masculine side. The first thing a trans girl in a hostile environment learns, even before she knows it's hostile, when everything is still pure intuition, is to control her eagerness or to fake it until not even she herself can tell if it's genuine. In that early part of the decade, the binary was fiercely constructed and defended. The androgynous splendor of the eighties was just a mirage that both stimulated our desires and made our longing more painful, being so present and yet so very far away. For me, a secret little trans girl in a working-class neighborhood, who had no idea what in the hell she would end up becoming, seeing Boy George in all his cheerful femininity or Prince in fishnet stockings was like seeing lightning bugs in a damp black cave. A flash of hope so fleeting that you weren't even sure it had existed.

The boldest section of The Girls stocked clothing inspired by the hedonistic cultural wave known as the Movida Madrileña, which to us was something we saw on TV, like *Anillos de oro* or *Dallas.* . . . Fiction about a world that wasn't ours. A wild carnival, alien to our human lives, that hovered over our reality there at the end of the number 7 metro line. Onscreen they said that Madrid was a city where boys in makeup danced till dawn; in San Blas, grown-ups would seriously debate whether it was worse for your son to be a drug addict or a faggot. They also talked about AIDS, everywhere, all the time, shifting between disgust, cruelty, shame, and pity in every conversation, predicting death sentences and loneliness for its sufferers. I listened intently, greedily, as if some invisible force were compelling me to eat black, moldy bread. I absorbed it all into the pit inside me and convinced myself that it was better to leave things as they were and save any possible confessions for when the world—or I—had changed.

Of course I wanted to go to The Girls! It was intoxicating to peek into that world of colors, mirrors, and dazzlingly colored lips. In that space, my mother, my aunts, the neighborhood women, momentarily set down the burden of their homes, their families, and their jobs; they set down their exhaustion and relaxed completely. They tried on blouses, skirts, three-quarter-length coats; they solicited advice from the salesgirls, who were extremely clever, loving, and knowledgeable about fashion.

The women would inspect themselves in the mirror carefully,

posing, complaining about their bodies, and receiving the perfect dose of validation from those professional salesgirls. It was always the same game, ending with a reduced-price skirt in a bag or a shirt with just a hint of lace they wouldn't have many chances to wear, but having it in the drawer, just in case, lifted their spirits.

How could I not want to be part of that joyful, wondrous world? How could I not want to blend in with that landscape? It was like filling my lungs with fresh air. I forgot all the darkness welling inside me. When the women entered that space, they bared an aspect of their nature that I found very moving. When they tried on clothes with explosive patterns, slight falls, and floaty skirts with flares and flounces, they transformed into enormous, strange, vivacious animals with iridescent coats, whose movements gave off a whiff of perfume and makeup, impregnating everything with a salty sisterhood that broke my little transvestite heart.

PEBBLE FACE

Margarita never entered The Girls. No one had said she couldn't, but she was aware of the prescribed limits of the world she was allowed to inhabit. She was the tallest woman in the neighborhood. In fact, she was the tallest woman I'd ever seen in my life. She was always perfectly coiffed despite dyeing and styling her own hair. She wore plenty of makeup and was escorted by a halo of perfume that heralded her arrival and remained a reminder once she'd gone. This was in contrast to her insistence on wearing a house-coat everywhere. It's true that she kept her housecoats spick-and-span, but you would expect a woman who took such care with her appearance to be dressed just as painstakingly. In her own way, she was careful about what she wore, and no one ever saw a stain on her pink housecoat or on her matching slippers, complete with a trim of pink fur at the end of the bridge and a discreet kitten heel.

I was obsessed with how women dressed. At home, we hoarded pretty much every society magazine published in Spain. I adopted some of my mother's allegiances and worshipped Caroline of Monaco, who was almost as perfect as Grace. Almost. I began to learn to identify fashion designers' names with their garments, and recognized the silhouettes of their designs and the bodies they designed for. Borrowing from the women on those magazine pages, I dreamed of being dressed by Manuel Piña: striking, voluminous, strange, feminine, and defined. I spent my days imagining, but I was incapable of projecting my own image into the future, as if what I was, who I was, were condemned to a perpetual childhood, playing hide-and-seek with existence.

Margarita was my first contact with that future projection, which was why I couldn't stand her.

Her face was disfigured by protrusions that covered her cheekbones and cheeks almost entirely, blisters that seemed filled with hardened liquid, that looked bumpy and probably felt that way, too. As if someone had slipped rocks under her skin. Those bumps compromised her vision, constricting her line of sight and forcing her to lean forward to focus, adopting a posture and angle that weren't particularly flattering.

She made me uncomfortable, like a Ghost of Christmas Yet to Come. My thoughts continued to reject any precise outline of self-acceptance. But that wasn't something I could fight against; all I could do was hide until one day it blew up in my face. My life and my sentimental education matured within a desperately sad privacy where I kept doing things in secret. I grew up having to appear to be something I wasn't, which I got better and better at doing, which became more painful with each passing day, as I became more convinced that my world, the world that was incessantly slipping away, was the world of women. As puberty approached and I resisted facing reality, the outlines of my suffering merged into a ghastly foursome of depersonalization, denial, escaping, and lies, forming a persistent, sustained hum that was driving me mad, a buzzing in my ears that somehow managed to articulate words of contempt.

Margarita was a stab of reality knocking at the door. Confirmation of what I didn't want to see or know about. When I peeked into my garden of famous transvestites and transsexuals—because while I could deny it to myself three times a day, I still hungered for role models—it turned out they were all of the same ilk. They seemed otherworldly: opalescent, colossal, and fascinating. Sylvester, Bibi, Amanda Lear, Tula Cossey, Cris Miró. I didn't dare consider that this was what I wanted my life to be, despite a prick of euphoria filling my chest when I looked at them. I couldn't want that. Everything I had heard said about them was framed by the language used for describing sickness, along with words of affliction and shame. Sometimes there was admiration, but it wasn't admiration of something marvelous but more like the applause after a play or at some costume party. Something considered entertaining as ostentatious spectacle, with no inherent beauty beyond its skillful artifice. The worst were the mocking words that came after a couple of stiff drinks, the ones used on television in comedies or family programs, jokes that made me want to vomit. I searched everywhere for a language of pride and strength so that I could finally fucking explain myself, but I couldn't locate it no matter how hard I tried. As a little girl, I wasn't afraid to think about being like this or fantasize about it; what terrified me was other people's reactions, the way they spoke about something so lovely. The contempt in their voices, the repulsion they seemed to feel. It was those overheard conversations, the ones you pretend not to be listening to, that convinced me I was a deviant creature who had to hide away.

The days when I tried to overcome my fear and define myself, even if only in a whisper, in front of the bathroom mirror—my accomplice—the only words I had were the ones I had heard others speak. No matter how cleverly I spun them, I couldn't find the right combination that defined me with the justice I deserved, and instead I ended up sketching out a walking, breathing mistake.

I didn't know where Margarita and her bumps had come from, but they obviously weren't from the same realm as those goddesses in the magazines and music videos who had conquered femininity with such panache. It couldn't be. It was impossible. Bibi's skin was smooth, Amanda's face was angular and perfect, Sylvester gleamed as if made of crystal, and Tula and Cris were so pretty, it hurt a bit to look at them. Yet none of them were spared derision. They were unquestionably women, so attractive that people quickly felt they had to say loud and clear that "they were men." As if saying those words would revoke the demon of desire in whoever uttered them.

Women like Margarita were the targets of jokes that made my throat catch; they were the caricatures, the ones imitated with very deep voices, the ones whose mere presence made me suffer because they granted the entire world license to humiliate us with no remorse. I didn't realize that Margarita and my goddesses were one and the same, women who had secured a small or large space of freedom by fighting tooth and nail, and that was what made them so terrifying. The example they set. I wasn't aware of any of that then; I didn't have the slightest idea of what true beauty was. That was why I pleaded with my mother's God, if He was listening, to not give me Margarita's same fate. I swore allegiance to any higher power, sacrilege be damned, if they would just spare me the lot of the grotesque women.

THE LONELY WOMEN

Margarita was always very friendly when we ran into her. If I was with my parents, she would usually stop to speak with them and look at me sweetly, as if reading in my face definitions I couldn't even give myself. That connection between us, which was obvious, made me ill. I became obsessed with the idea that I had a little flame floating over my head, like the one I'd seen over the apostles in my illustrated Bible but that was visible only to faggots, dykes, whores, and trannies. Not only did I exhibit the natural grace of a boiled ham, but it turned out a violet flame was outing me as a ladyboy on the lower astral plane.

Margarita was devoted body and soul to her mother, who was elderly and completely dependent on her. Margarita was proud to keep her clean "as a whistle," she would always say. To have her mother's "meals ready right on time" and to make sure she never missed a doctor's appointment or a pill. We would see them strolling through the neighborhood, mother gripping daughter's arm, to run brief errands, as much as her mother's crippled legs could take, which wasn't much at all.

I knew that Margarita was trans, obviously, very early on. My father explained it to me in curt but kind words without being hurtful or insulting, something that was a comfort to some sensitive spot in my heart, something that I was able to appreciate much later. That's how my father was. He always told us the truth, without beating around the bush, and he believed we had the right to answers. For a man born in those silent years after the civil war, he was unprejudiced, and in his way—which was molded by his environment, his generation, and how he was raised—he was pretty open-minded. Less intolerant than you would expect of a man in his circumstances.

As for the fact that Margarita was trans, it wasn't dwelt on much in the neighborhood, even though everyone knew. She was treated with some respect to her face, but later, behind her back, the tongues grew bolder and crueler. The term "trans" didn't yet exist; in the best cases, they used "transsexuals," and in the worst, slurs that survive to this century.

Although she was mostly tolerated, Margarita still had to face insensitive malice. She always tried to purchase her cigarettes at the same tobacco shop, run by twin brothers who looked sickly and acted like cretins. They'd inherited the business from their father, an informant for the fascist regime, who had also passed down his buggy eyes and greenish skin. Margarita would go in, ask for her brand, and they would often say they'd run out, even though a conspicuous tower of packs stood behind the partition. They made sure to do it when nobody was around so that they could deny it, pleading affliction, crossing their hands over their chests like Saint Gemma Galgani if anyone asked. Because the whole neighborhood ended up hearing about stuff like this, and they would make inquiries. Those were the kind of petty cruelties Margarita had to suffer every once in a while. Maybe because of her age or because of the hidden fury some presumed she had, she was treated with the apprehension afforded a sphinx or a chimera. She wasn't a victim of brutal violence the way faggots, dykes, and young transsexuals were; in her case, it was expressed as entombed coldness.

She wasn't subjected to constant derision, but she was never just another woman. Her behavior had to be exemplary. She couldn't cause any problems—a standard that was interpreted very loosely. She went to Mass every Sunday, but afterwards, she didn't linger in front of the church door. That was one of the invisible borders that was abundantly clear to her. Her reward was comments like "Have to give her credit; Margarita knows her place" or "Truth is, she lives her life and doesn't bother anybody," as if being a trans woman was an imposition in and of itself, one she had to temper by keeping quiet, being nicer than anybody else, and not responding to provocations. I surmised that, and my lungs shriveled every time I noticed it. I realized how small her world was and how much effort went into ensuring it shrunk slowly. The walls of my skin, my entire body, already felt claustrophobic, a diving suit that kept me isolated at the depths of a dead sea. The thought of ending up like her forever—imagining my lungs getting smaller, my skin shrinking, and my heart compressed almost to collapsing—was terrifying.

The exemplariness demanded of Margarita had to do with acquiescence.

Of course, Margarita was exemplary.

She always had a "Honey" on the tip of her tongue and was always primed to help out, carry shopping bags, hold the door, or run errands for whoever crossed her path. She didn't mind picking up an extra pound of tangerines so a neighbor wouldn't have to go to the store. The kids hooked on heroin called her "Mamarita"; she would buy them bread, cheap cold cuts, milkshakes, and chocolate puff pastries to get them through the day. She didn't give them money because she didn't have any to spare and, because she knew how to treat them, nobody would have thought to mug her. They shared a camaraderie, one she didn't have with the rest of the neighborhood. Whether it was out of self-interest or real affection, they treated her with respect and were never threatening. Even when withdrawal was eating them alive and they couldn't even control their sphincters, they never demanded anything of her, although sometimes they did beg.

Much older women, of her mother's age, were less severe in their demands and granted her some sort of a station. Most of them had already been mothers during the civil war. They were less prejudiced, or at least in a different way. They were impressed by her self-sacrifice, the delicacy with which she carried out her duties as a daughter. Those things seemed to guarantee that she was a pillar of the community, that they could count on her. Every day she would administer an insulin injection to Señora Reme, her widowed neighbor across the hall and the mother of two dead sons; one fell from the fourth floor of a construction site and the other drowned in heroin. Margarita would also rub down another neighbor, Mamerta the Headbutter, with rosemary extract, or vinegar when that was all they had. Mamerta could hardly move after debilitating arthritis left her legs and hands deformed. Her nickname had followed her from her old hood, Comillas, because she'd headbutted a handsy Falangist a couple of months before the war ended, leaving him unconscious. From all accounts, she'd been an indomitable woman who refused to bow to any man. They said that she'd stubbornly taken on very demanding physical jobs, "men's work," all her life, because they paid better and because she could. Until one day, her body cried uncle, and she ended up shuttered at home, dependent on the kindness of neighbors.

Margarita was welcome in the homes of lonely women. The ones who couldn't afford the luxury of refusing a selfless hand.

Via the small courtesies that Margarita conferred them, they'd woven a network of loneliness that lightened their loads. They knew how one's sugar levels were, how another's legs were doing, and yet another's blood pressure readings. In the summer, they would sit out in the cooler air of the doorway. Margarita would bring out the chairs of those who couldn't do it for themselves, placing her mother in one, and remain amid the group but standing, not saying much, leaning against the wall of the building with her little pack of sunflower seeds, her cigarettes, and her thoughts somewhere far away.

I couldn't take my eyes off her. She was my attraction to the void, and the void wore a housecoat and lipstick. I analyzed everything she did and seemed to develop a sixth sense for when she was leaving the house. We would often meet on my way back from school, when she was headed in the opposite direction to go clean somewhere. She would smile at me. I would turn my face away or lower my gaze, but then turn to watch her walk off. Sometimes she would look back suddenly and catch me staring. She would smile again and continue on her way.

She was the source of all my fears, and at the same time, her presence lightened my burden, as if we shared a limited bubble of air, and she would ration most of it for me until I learned to hold my breath. I found her ability to do that comforting and terrifying; it made me feel exposed.

Margarita earned a living as a cleaner. She'd been a whore before that. My father told me that too, without making a big deal about it; we'd been around women in the oldest profession for all our lives. On the third floor, two of our neighbors, Señora Agustina and Merceditas, mother and daughter, used their apartment as both living space and the headquarters of their little sex business. Their apartment had the same size and distribution as ours, and they took turns using the smallest room for work. While one of them was with a customer, the other would scrub and mop. It always smelled like pine cleaning solution through their door, which, since it occupied the top floor, would send the aroma cascading down the entire staircase. They had a parrot who would shriek, "Rascal! Raasscal!" every time some man would come in or out of their place. The flow of clients was discreet but constant. Occasionally one of them would even say hi as they passed us by on the lower steps, where the kids in the building would play and hang out, and when that happened, the client would get a real earful. Those charming women had one hard-and-fast condition for access to their services: leave the children alone and don't say a word to them. I always knew what they were and what they did, and I never thought of whores as being different from other women.

When the years started to weigh heavily on Margarita's mother and she couldn't do it all on her own, Margarita quit that job to come back home and take care of her. In any case, the bars on Calle Orense, where she solicited most of her clients, were disappearing in the late eighties. Her own age made it difficult to make a living in the parks like when she started out—too many hours on her feet for a body that had already weathered so much. I tried to imagine her young, and even though it was hard to distance her current appearance, with her size and her lanky-bird body language, she must have been remarkable. The truth is, she still was. Although it became harder and harder for me, I preferred to see her as distant and ugly, if only to preserve my fantasies of fairylike transformation. One day, I would cease to inhabit the suffocating, frightened depths and would blossom like a perfect fairy, a winged creature of the air. Margarita, with her scars and her mundaneness, with her invisible limits, represented the opposite of all that. She was the trans equivalent of finding out that it was your parents, and not the Three Kings, who brought your Christmas presents. I refused to accept that we were creatures from the same forest, despite my obsession with gaping at her from behind every bend of our brick-and-tar neighborhood like a lovestruck pixie.

"Margarita came by the factory looking for work," my father said to my mother at lunch one day.

Hearing her name, I perked up and widened my eyes. Anything that had to do with her was a magnet for my attention. My parents must have noted my oversized interest, but they never pointed it out to me. Maybe a puzzled look was exchanged between them, but I never bothered to decipher it.

"And what did you tell her? You already have a cleaning lady."

My mother knew that Margarita was constantly hunting for work wherever she could find it. She never said no to anything. They had that in common, and somehow that made my mother worry. It appealed to her sense of camaraderie. She recognized in herself that same need, that same drive.

"And what could I tell her, Jimena? I sent her over to talk to Remedios, who's the one who makes those decisions. But they're not gonna fire Nieves. She's been with us for three or four years already, and she does good work. They talked for a while and then went together over to the next warehouse, the one with the wood, to ask there."

"What kind of work is she looking for?" I pried.

"Cleaning, son, what else?" my mother snapped, as if the question was about her. She reacted with the damaged self-esteem of cleaners, whose hard work always goes unrecognized. "And don't eat any more croquettes; they're really fattening. I'll cut you up some fruit," she added, with the same cloaked outrage as when she'd talked about Margarita's failed attempt to find work. She never missed a chance to mention how much I ate.

That usually made me feel very embarrassed, but I was so invested in their conversation about Margarita that it rolled right off my back. I handed the croquette to my brother, who accepted it with a complicit shrug and gulped it down to curb the awkwardness as soon as possible.

"What did the wood guys say? Because that Patxi is a real cheapskate," my mother said.

"What do I know? It's not like I followed them. He must've said no, he'd rather wait until it bursts into flame than pay someone to clean that warehouse. I can just see him, running out, on fire, with his fucking mother still inside. The sawdust in there dates from the year of the flood."

"She'll find something. Truth is, she's got balls. She works like a mule, Margarita does."

My mother declared it with some pride. She couldn't help siding with Margarita, both of them cleaners, and she spoke of her the same way she always spoke about her own capacity for hard work, making it clear she gave it her all. "If I gotta get down on my knees, I will; if I gotta scrub like a bat outta hell, I will, but it'll be clean when I'm done." I'd heard her say that a while back during another discussion, and I'd never forgotten it. It could be her epitaph.

"Why doesn't she go back to being a whore?" I didn't yet understand the demands of such work, but I asked the question perfectly aware of what I was saying. Being a whore seemed like a decent option, and since she'd been one in the past, she must've known what she was doing.

"Hold on a minute, what's it to you? That's her business, and you need to listen with your mouth shut. Always looking for trouble, this one. We're talking to each other, me and your mother. Besides, Margarita doesn't have the age or the stamina anymore to be standing all day and all night, especially when it gets cold."

Even though my father scolded me for what he considered excessive curiosity about a subject that was out of my league, he never left me wondering. He'd always tack on an answer to my questions. I kept it to myself, but I was thinking—as I gnawed on a slice of melon—that it was the same difference to wait out in the cold on the street as to be mopping up freezing warehouses at dawn before the workers arrived. I knew about that because that was my mother's livelihood and because I would often visit my dad at his work site, a huge industrial building with very bad insulation. In the winter, people worked there with coats on, and through the summer they managed with cool water and prayers for the best.

THE SAME FOREST

All of a sudden, I stopped seeing Margarita so often. She left the house less, and when she did, she seemed to always be in a rush. We no longer crossed paths on my way home from school, and I didn't see her wandering around the industrial park in her constant pilgrimages in search of some odd morsel of work so she could cobble together enough to put hot meals on the table. Her classic bun was more disheveled than usual, and very thin wisps of hair fell around her face. For the first time, her hair was more gray than blond, and her lips paler than her cheeks.

She did always offer a good morning or a good afternoon, and she bought more groceries than usual to keep from having to go out as much. And so the days passed, and a few whole seasons, without us seeing much of her.

I missed her. Every day on my way back from school, I would hope to see her coming around a corner with her crane's gait. But it didn't happen, leaving me feeling strangely alone. I asked those same higher powers I used to pray to, to not be like Margarita, now in a whisper, to bring her back to me at least a couple of times a week. Maybe just a brief encounter at the newspaper stand where we both stocked up on magazines every week. I was sent by my mother; she and Margarita both collected them.

I was too ashamed to ask at home about her. My interest in Margarita could force me to give explanations or be branded a gossip again, which I was already starting to tire of. As observant and clever as I imagined myself to be, I didn't know how to read my neighborhood. Spending my entire life feeling alienated from those people, hiding from them behind an elaborate lie in the shape of a chubby, nice, know-it-all boy, had deprived me of the right to understand them. If there was some rumor or whisper network intel on the streets of San Blas about what was going on with Margarita, I wasn't in on it. All trans girls grow up alone.

One very early morning in late winter, one of those mornings when the first rays of sun gleam on the frost and the resulting light makes everything chime, I was awoken by the buzzing of my parents whispering in the next room. I was perfectly familiar with the register they used to discuss something happening on the street, the register of curtains drawn open. Our neighborhood was filled with scenes that could be viewed from the house: violent scenes; amusing scenes; sad, absurd scenes; all sorts. I got out of bed and looked out the window. A brown van was parked on the sidewalk, right in front of Margarita's door. After a short while during which even the air was stock-still, a couple of men showed up wheeling a bright white stretcher. There was a covered body on it, a small body taking up little space, a body of almost childlike dimensions. Behind it marched Margarita, distraught, as if in a procession, but without the agitation I usually associated with death. She walked tall, solemnly, slowly, satisfied with just touching her fingers to the end of the stretcher, near the covered feet of her mother, Doña Ana.

"Please, why won't you let me put some clothes on her? It won't take long at all." If a broken heart could speak, it would've sounded exactly like Margarita as she pleaded with them. By this point, a lot of us were looking out our windows or watching from the street, silent as a frozen lake.

"Look, *Señor* Jiménez, we already told you. We have to take her away like this. Talk to the judge if you want, but the medical examiners have to have a look at her."

That "señor" issued from the lips of a miserable pencil pusher—dirt-poor but emboldened by petty authority—brought bile to my throat. I was discovering who I was through that sort of gut punch, words that lodged deep within me and were impossible to forget. Before you get the chance to define yourself, others trace your outline with their prejudices and their aggressions. I clenched my fists until my fingernails left indents on my palms. I tried to hold back my tears, but I've never been able to silence my sobs to this day.

Margarita didn't even flinch; her entire face was already crushed, as if gravity were pulling harder on her than on anyone else, and her bumpy face had to bear all the world's weight. Just another "señor." For someone who had been through Franco's interrogation rooms, the Law on Social Danger, and male prisons, it was a mere scratch on hardened leather.

"What about if I give you a little bag with her clothes folded up inside, just a little bag? Can someone dress her once they've finished the examination?"

The tenderest question in the history of the world. Margarita needed to wash and dress her mother one last time, comb her hair, moisturize her knotty little hands. Margarita needed to say her farewell by caring for her mother, slowly carrying out her daily routine, knowing it would be the last time. Margarita had performed that ritual for years with irreproachable love and devotion. For her mother and for herself. A final gesture of caretaking was a way for her to say goodbye to a part of her own life. A ritual that would put an end to the shared intimacy so Margarita could begin to think about recovering her own once she'd taken the time to grieve.

"That's up to the insurance guys, Señor Jiménez."

"Please, don't call me señor. It's just that we don't have insurance."

"Shoulda thought of that sooner, señor. Too late for crying now."

That guy had no shame; all that was required of him was to carry out the honorable job of removing corpses from homes or the street with the utmost respect, or at least in silence, and he was smacking Margarita across the face in front of everybody. That was the first time I saw—with total clarity—that specific humiliation of denying someone their name, of exposing someone's vulnerability and turning them into a joke, of crushing any personal achievements or history, no matter how painful, just to be able to flaunt power. In that moment, I felt myself so powerfully part of a tribe that it seemed it was my birthright. All my ghosts, all my fears, put their cold hands on my back, on my neck, on my guts, on my crotch, on my eyes, and they all squeezed at the same time. I was afraid for Margarita, and I was afraid for myself. We did belong in the same forest; we did share a terrible and lovely complicity. Margarita was pretty, and I had been blind and swallowed up by the reveries of a childish fear of life. I had a flash of María the Wig and the grooves in her skin, the way her scarred face set limits and commanded respect, even if by fear or merely banishing the jeers to far, far away. Margarita's face before that asshole bureaucrat, demolished by pain, more swollen than ever after sustained sobbing, that face that tugged at my chest, seemed the image of dignity, of strength, the face of a woman who had crossed Tartarus without needing rescue because she had conquered hell. I understood that those bulging bits of poorly applied silicone that surfaced on her face were the remains of her search for beauty, which in her day, she'd yearned for just as I yearned for it, with the same thirst and the same desperation. Being like her wasn't a curse; it was a gift. Bearing that stigmata so visibly meant having aspired to brush up against the sublime. I wanted to kiss every bump on her face tenderly, like a novice would kiss her Mother Superior on her ordination day.

"Heyyyy now, mister, don't you think you're overstepping? Who do you think you are to speak to a lady like that?"

Sebastián was an imposing man, hardened by work and used to challenging authority ever since he set foot in this world. He was a street fruit vendor, although he never turned down odd jobs as a bricklayer, plumber, carpenter, or painter. He was one of those people who knew how to do everything. Always dressed in black, winter and summer, in the same shirt with the sleeves rolled halfway up his forearms, as far as the girth of his muscles permitted. His thick, pointed black beard made me think of the illustrations in my mythology books. Sebastián was Ajax. Enormous, powerful, sarcastic, and possessed of a rage he chose to display only on very rare occasions because it was so terrible.

"What'd you say?"

That was the civil servant's response, but he could have said anything just as easily. He'd heard Sebastián perfectly and was only trying to buy time. Everyone heard how his voice was trembling. It was incredible how quickly violent men turned tail. He hurriedly pushed the stretcher into the cargo compartment, closed it right away, and headed casually to the front of the van.

"I said why are you speaking like that to a lady in front of her mother's dead body. Didn't you learn respect at home, or am I gonna have to teach it to you myself?"

"Listen, leave me alone. I have work to do." His voice could barely be heard. His previous little field-marshal tone had been reduced to the lowest piece of shit in the barracks in front of the entire neighborhood.

"Fucking hell, I do, too. But that's not what I'm talking about. Before you leave, you have to apologize to Señora Margarita."

Sebastián was speaking very firmly but with the calm of someone who knew he was in charge. He wasn't going to allow any room for humiliation; he knew it firsthand from how they confiscated the fruit that was his livelihood, from the scorn hurled at his children at school, from the many times they reinspected the bills his wife paid with in stores. Sebastián had locked his jaws on that petty squib's spine, and he wasn't going to let him go.

"Do you want me to call the police? I've got a radio in the van, and they'll be here in a—"

"Turn around and apologize to the lady. This is your last warning!"

Everybody knew the loud voice Sebastián used to hawk his merchandise through the streets. This was not that voice. This was one we had rarely ever heard. Maybe in arguments with the police or when someone who'd hired him didn't hold up their end of the bargain, taking advantage of the fact that he was unlikely to report them since his kind had no chance before a judge. It was a voice that was in one's best interest to obey. The kind that doused any ember of violence in the person it was directed towards.

"Sebastián, honey, let it go." Margarita tried to mediate because smoothing raised hackles was in her very nature. She would've done it at her own execution.

"I'm not letting it go, Margarita. And I'm very sorry. Your mother was a good woman; my heart goes out to you. But nobody is leaving here until this man apologizes."

The small little man, who had started to sweat and continually wiped a handkerchief over his hairless head, stammered for a few seconds and retraced his steps until he was in front of Margarita, whom he addressed without making eye contact.

"Sorry, señora, I was just reading what it said on the card. I didn't mean to offend you."

It was more out of fear than shame, but he apologized.

His co-worker, who was the one driving, took his place behind the steering wheel, and the small man rushed back to the van, gripping a black file folder as if it were the last plank left of his shipwrecked boat.

"Wait a minute!" shouted someone from inside the open doorway. All heads turned to see who was yelling with such urgency. Just in case, Sebastián placed one hand on the door handle to the hearse van, so they weren't tempted to shut it and drive off. Asunción, a neighbor who'd dreamed of being a rumba singer but had ended up selling lottery tickets, whom everybody knew as Lil Crip because of a polio vaccine she never got, banged her crutch against the ground at a good pace, huffing and puffing. Not only was she running but in her free hand she waved a plastic bag as if it were a flag, which, with her physical handicap, was quite a feat.

"Ay, Asun! Ay!" Margarita very delicately took the bag and brought it up to her face to cover her sobs, which were bubbling up again.

"Open up the back, please!" yelled Margarita, her voice now desperate.

Sebastián placed his hand on the steering wheel.

"Please, do as the lady says and open up the back," he requested, with the gracious tone of a strict father.

The civil servants exchanged a couple of glances, weighing

the situation before deciding that the best course of action would be to give in and not make matters worse. The driver was the one who got out of the van and opened the cargo door.

Margarita pulled a perfectly folded black dress with lace trim at the neck from the plastic bag and placed it on the stretcher.

"Tell them to put it on you when they've finished, Mamá. Remember that the sleeves are a little tight, and they have to put your arms in slowly, or they'll tear. Forgive me; I didn't have time to mend it." Then she brought her head close to her hand on the white sheet, there where her mother's feet must have been, and she kissed her three or four times. When she'd finished her farewell, the hearse started up and left. The neighbor ladies came over to give Margarita their condolences and scattered one by one until the street was almost empty.

It was still a little while before the neighborhood would teem with activity. It was the time of day for freshly made coffee in the kitchen, with the radio news playing and the final silence of the morning before everything began to spin.

JAY

We'd met at the worst possible venue. A martial arts dojo we were both forced to attend, another such lame male rite of passage with little real-world applicability. If one of the reasons for practicing the incredibly boring sport that was karate was to develop martial abilities that, if need be, we could use to defend ourselves from possible aggression or, speaking bluntly, to learn how to beat the shit out of people with ease, it wasn't terribly effective. Living in a neighborhood that was demanding in terms of personal safety, a rough hood, taught you from a young age that any skinny, nervous kid accustomed to fighting every day could fuck up even the most experienced black belt, tae kwon do expert, or kung fu ace. I had no interest in any of it. I was never able to get into the mythos of the master and the apprentice, or the chi, or any of that philosophical dialectic that served as a cover-up for the appalling dynamics and hierarchies inside the dojo. I was bored and couldn't give two shits about that pretentious imitation of boot camp. I spent the classes, which dragged on forever, thinking about anything but. When I had no other choice but to pay attention because I had to fight, I made sure to inflict as much damage as I could right off the bat, disregarding the rules so I would be disqualified and banned from participating as a penalty. I couldn't care less about camaraderie. There was no trace left of the fumbling creature I'd been as a child. Everyone chalked that up to karate and an iron discipline in my food intake, but they had no idea the coordination and athletic fitness one cultivates from learning Madonna's choreographed dance moves.

Every last one.

I would dance in my room whenever I got the chance. Furiously, as if I were sparring with the air around me, and at the same time, being as feminine as I could, which was very. Almost everything I did in life back then stemmed from a place of rage and angst. My body was changing and starting to really repulse me. I was growing stronger by the month, my voice deepening so fast that I didn't even realize it until someone mentioned it when I answered the phone. I usually had to stifle a sob to keep speaking naturally. I was even starting to develop facial hair, which would later become my worst enemy. The disgust I was feeling towards my body had evolved from when I was a child. Before, it had to do with feeling very far from something unachievable, something beautiful and ethereal, as if I were chained to an earthly reality from which the moon was always unreachable, but now there was an added feeling of deformity and distension. I saw myself as a vessel of dead skin that was sprouting protuberances, as if I had loose bones inside that randomly crossed swords, bulging around tensions. I wore enormous clothes to conceal what I understood as a body that was putrefying from one season to the next.

When I couldn't dance, I ran, using the same music as a soundtrack for the two activities, both of which I practiced compulsively. You don't know what moving with teenage desperation is until you dance to "Papa Don't Preach" at full blast, or what escapism is until you run with "Cemetry Gates" by The Smiths on your Walkman. I was in love with Morrissey. Depeche Mode also took me far away, and The Cure and Elton John made me cry like when I would look at myself in the mirror, trying to find something to love. I danced, I ran, and I fled; I only wanted to escape.

Flee to him. To Jay.

The first time I saw him, in the gym locker room, I blushed so hard that someone asked if I was okay. I had to feign a sudden urge to use the bathroom to justify my panicked expression and to regain my composure. He, who had the most piercing sideways glance I've ever known, caught the whole scene.

He was the son of an American officer stationed at the To-rrejón Air Base and a French teacher. He'd been raised in Sacramento, Manila, and Paris, and God knows that, at seventeen, he hadn't wasted any time.

I liked to think that we had recognized each other in that first glance, but the truth is, he was the one who knew how to see. He was supersmart, self-assured, and deployed an endless catalogue of subtle provocations. He barely spoke Spanish, just what he'd learned in California and the Philippines, but he never had any problem conveying whatever he wanted to say.

From that very first look, anytime our eyes met in the locker room, I would spend the next hour with the chills and all the fantasies a bookish teenager could dream up. Looking at him when he wasn't looking at me was even worse; it felt like I'd reached a dirty, suffocating, narcotic state. I wanted to punch him and have him strike back three times harder. I wanted him to embrace me slowly and whisper things I didn't understand into my ear, as if he truly loved me.

It wasn't either of those things, but it was something. He would seek me out on the tatami when we had to do partner exercises. He would change his clothes beside me before and after class. We would laugh as we tried to understand each other in different languages. He paid a lot of attention to me, with his eyes open very wide and his head tilted to one side like a fawn listening to the wind. His body language drove me wild;

it was arousing and comfortable, effeminate and athletic, long, gentle, and able to tense like steel. He was like a dancer from ancient Persia. He was Bagoas, the boy who seduced Alexander the Great. When I was with him, I felt I could say anything. After much difficulty, we started to see each other outside of that ridiculous environment. I don't know what excuse he used, considering how far away he lived and that his father wasn't exactly the type to accept just any explanation. Lieutenant Nichols gave his son very little breathing room, although Jay astutely took advantage of every bit. I would say I was going to play role-playing games, basketball, or take a walk, the kind of vagueness your parents accepted if they saw you as male, and you never got in trouble, and your grades were fine.

Jay had no patience, and there was no hand-holding, no slow progression. The first time we were alone together, we met up in front of one of the side doors of Our Lady of Almudena Cemetery, the one opposite the entrance to the civil cemetery. That was a no-man's-land with just a very narrow two-way paved street running past, and all you could see were the old, crumbling brick walls of the necropolis. The sidewalks glued to the wall were scant and very poorly maintained, covered in cracks, as if those shot by firing squad there during the civil war banged against the ground to keep from being forgotten. They were so narrow, two people couldn't walk side by side comfortably. The place was deserted. We'd barely entered the area with the oldest graves when he grabbed me by my belt loop, pulled me towards him, and kissed me on the lips. The first thing I thought was how brave he was. I never would have dared do something like that without being completely sure—understood as a signed declaration before witnesses and a competent authority—that the person in front of me wanted me to kiss them. The idea of rejection, of the possible violence and ridicule, often kept me up at night.

I couldn't imagine any of the teenage boys I knew taking an advance from me well, no matter how respectful it was. If I had acted with them the way they acted with girls, I would have found myself waking up bruised and swollen in an empty lot somewhere. That thought wasn't an exaggeration; it was conditioning. Daniel, the shoemaker's son, a distant neighbor but an acquaintance of my older cousins, a sweet, kind boy whose body language was blessed with a lovely swish, came home one early Saturday morning with a broken jaw, missing a finger on his right hand, and his face smeared with red lipstick. From that night on, he never went out alone, and he ended up requesting a disability pension due to the trauma of what was meant to be his first date. He was fifteen years old. That kiss Jay gave me, so perfect, so soft, so warm, was slow to reach the place inside me where such things are received. That kiss, my first, was prefaced by a rush of thoughts of every horror story I had witnessed or heard in my life about people like me. They were there with me, translucent and frozen, those who'd survived and those who hadn't. I saw Daniel, the shoemaker's beautiful son; I saw Alicia, a fantastic girl who used to play soccer on the neighborhood pitches in a Rayo Vallecano jersey, who laughed really loudly when she scored a goal. A big, free laugh that was impossible to forget. They kicked her out of the house at fourteen because she was caught hugging another girl in the doorway. Yes, at fourteen. She wasn't even old enough to get into the movie theater alone. She had barely set foot outside her home when the world swallowed her whole. I also saw Benjamín, a distant relative, the son of my mother's second cousin, an aspiring dancer and actor, gorgeous as a big cat, my pied piper on Calle Amposta, who caught so much shit from his father and his brothers for being gay that all that was left of him was a trembling alcoholic who vanished from the neighborhood one summer night at the age of seventeen.

It wasn't fair that I showed up to such a special moment, my first kiss ever, with all that baggage. Our lives weren't like other people's, and they never would be. An interminable procession of ghosts was going to haunt us for the rest of our days and watch over our every step with a parting expression.

"You like good?" asked Jay, with mistaken words but with such perfect, charming delivery that it set off my bad habit of crying over everything.

"Yes, me like good. Kiss me more, please."

BEYOND SAN BLAS

J ay looked out for me and took care of me, but he wasn't wasting footage. Our dates were brief: before I knew it, I was on my way back home with my whole body screaming for relief but with the feeling that I'd abruptly awoken from a lovely dream. Over time, I understood that the brevity of our rendezvous followed a security protocol we had to put in place to avoid problems. We almost always saw each other in out-of-the-way but public places or amid enough squalor that we would go under the radar. I was fourteen years old, and I wouldn't turn fifteen with him still in my arms. I longed for a bit more tenderness after our impulses were sated. Of course, I wanted a confidant, a love, someone who, after sex, continued to caress my body, his hands defining it in better terms than I did with my poisoned gaze, but in those years, in that life of ours, there was no space for other sorts of tenderness that weren't purely carnal. There was definitely plenty of carnal tenderness, though.

Jay managed to find out about Chueca before I did. That neighborhood in the city center scared everyone, but for us, it was more or less a safe harbor. There was something going on there that was changing everything. I had no idea; I had barely ever been to the center, and exclusively with my parents, at Christmastime or some other special occasion, maybe a wedding, things like that. My life had unfolded between San Blas and a few summers in Cáceres and Alicante.

Jay wanted us to go to Chueca and check it out. Spending a whole afternoon together without fear of getting caught touching, without our hearts constantly in our throats, would be a dream come true. It was worth a shot.

Frightened people said it was a neighborhood of whores, drug addicts, and faggots who would mug you, and that, even if it was changing, it still wasn't a good place to let your guard down. From my perspective, growing up in the Great San Blas, that was laughable. In the seventies and eighties, people said similar things about my hood, and even though it could be a rough place, it wasn't what I'd call hell. At least, not for the reasons that gave it that reputation. They also talked about Villaverde that way, and Carabanchel, and Aluche. It didn't take a rocket scientist to understand that all of them were low-income, working-class neighborhoods. Each had organized politically only to be harshly punished for it, with the introduction of waves of heroin before being maligned in the wake of the drug's ravaging. They were also neighborhoods where gypsies lived, comfortable among equals, among workers, among poor folk. Gypsies were never allowed to just live, burdened with the reputation of ruining every place they move through and every place they settle in. They weren't guaranteed even the most basic rights as citizens, and even then, they were blamed for living with the scraps left to them. Chueca couldn't be that bad. I imagined a place smaller, denser, and with fewer families resembling families than in my neighborhood. People often forgot that junkies were somebody's kids and that whores were also mothers, daughters, and sisters.

One day, we went to Café Figueroa, on the corner of Calle de Augusto Figueroa and Hortaleza; it was spacious, comfortable, and filled with smoke. It was nothing like the cafés in my neighborhood, or any I'd ever seen. There were only men inside, of all ages. Even though they struck me as very old, they weren't, not really. It was the first time I saw men in pairs sitting next to each other when there was more space at the table. Even those things we think of as random, like the positions we take around a table in public, are actually governed by strict social norms. Those men sat together because they so desired. Outside of that café, it would have been unthinkable.

Jay was the one who'd discovered that such a place existed. As the years passed, I realized that, in addition to seeing me, he must have been gallivanting around with older, more experienced people. He knew too much for a seventeen-year-old recent arrival, and it wasn't easy to find out where to go and with whom. I didn't realize it at the time, but I profited from it. It was incredible to relinquish control and be able to focus on gathering up sensations that I thought were proscribed for me. I had already internalized trans fatalism and convinced myself that a life of loneliness awaited me. I was sure that I'd be trapped in a closet for a long time, pursuing relations with men and with women to reinforce my lie and end up alone, tormented by what could never be. The very few stories of women like me that I had seen and read always ended that same way. Even the all-powerful emcee in *Cabaret* spends the entire movie without a name and winds up in front of an audience filled with Nazis as a drumroll accompanies a firing squad.

Which is why Jay was a miracle, a gift from the heavens that wasn't going to come around again and that I had to squeeze for every last drop.

A laughing man came over to our table.

"What's this, no school today? You two should be playing hide-and-seek; what are you doing here?!"

I was dying of embarrassment, not knowing what to say. It was my first time, besides running errands in my neighborhood, being in a commercial establishment of any kind without my parents. I wasn't expecting to have to order something or talk with people. I looked to Jay, hoping he would take care of it, but, well . . . his Spanish was improving, but he was still no Cervantes. That was the kind of situation that made me start stuttering again, something I had mostly put behind me, so long as I was calm and could find the proper cadence.

"Yes, we are doing hide-and-seek," said Jay with aplomb and a good dose of insolence in his expression. I stared at him, wondering if his resources really were infinite. Not only had he known how to answer with the same wink the waiter had used, improvising a new innuendo, he also seemed to know the right tone for a conversation that I saw as a complete uphill climb. There were indications that that world would become mine, but it wasn't mine yet.

"Well, you're a clever little maricón, aren't you? And we say 'play-ing,' playing hide-and-seek. Not doing hide-and-seek." Jay nodded, and they both laughed.

"Careful with this one; she's been around the block, and you look like a real chicken." The waiter gently lifted my face by the chin to look into my eyes as he said it.

"You, hide-and-seek, take care of her for me; she's still just a baby. All right, what can I get you? All out of chocolate milk. How about some light coffees?"

We nodded. That was the first coffee I ever drank in my life.

We had sat down facing each other and stretched our arms over the table to interlace our fingers. Only those who'd learned to fear the public space and be ashamed to occupy it freely could understand what I was experiencing in that moment. The sensations were the same as fear but inverted, as if they were taking place above water when up until then I'd only known life down in the depths. I wanted to cry with joy and sadness. The parade of ghosts watched me from outside the café, through the windows; I didn't know whether the distant astral plane of fairies, transvestites, dykes, and bisexuals had opened up to celebrate that perfect slice of life with me, or whether they were there to remind me of my future place among them.

"Watch out for the boogeyman!" I took my hand out of Jay's and drew back my arm as if my shoulder was spring-loaded. The waiter, who was placing our coffees on the table, laughed his ass off. So did Jay.

"Relax, maricón! Sorry, baby girl, I couldn't help myself; seeing you two so cute and cozy, I just had to bust your balls a little. Let me know if you need anything else." He left the cups of coffee and went back the way he'd come.

"He's so nice, but he really gave me a scare. I like this place a lot. Thanks for bringing me here."

I was very nervous, but I also wanted time to stop and for that afternoon to never end. That was so like me: always thinking about the end of something lovely that had barely just begun.

"Yeah, he's funny," said Jay. "And your face, more funny."

"Hey, don't make fun of me, the waiter said you need to treat me good, that I'm just a baby and still green."

Jay had taken "baby girl" to mean something other than small and young and, really, he wasn't that far off track. The green part he didn't get at all.

"Look, with 'baby girl,' he was just talking about my age, that I'm very young, you understand?"

"Yes, and what about 'green'?"

We interlaced our fingers again.

"Like fruit that hasn't ripened." He looked at me very carefully, but my fruit explanation still confused him. "When you eat a piece of fruit and it's bitter, still green-colored, as if it was a plant instead of a fruit, because it was picked from the tree too soon, you know?"

"Yes."

"With people, it's the same thing, they say someone's green to refer to ... to describe ... to talk about someone who doesn't have a lot of experience, because they're young or haven't seen much of the world."

"And you green as maricón, then." I almost spat out my mouthful of coffee.

"Yes, stupid, I green as maricón." Kissing in the middle of a burst of laughter was an experience that, as soon as it was happening, I promised myself to never forget.

We kept on chatting without letting go of each other's hands, moving closer and closer. Antonio left us alone even though we had finished our coffees quickly and were occupying a table without ordering anything else. I wanted to think that he was enjoying watching us. Many years later, I understood that for as limited and sometimes dark our queer youth was, we savored a silver lining that Antonio's generation, who I then figured was in his early forties, didn't have.

At fourteen, I saw nothing wrong with having sporadic, furtive sex in secluded locations. Thanks to our Círculo de Lectores subscription, I'd devoured books by Terenci Moix and Eduardo Mendicutti. I'd also read Gerald Walker, and I'd memorized every frame of Almodóvar's *Labyrinth of Passion*. My parents let me read whatever I wanted; I spent so many hours in the pages of books, and it seemed to make me so happy that they never argued about the titles. I watched certain movies either in secret or just discreetly, making sure I was alone. They weren't big fans of the silver screen; my brother went out a lot, and I often had our family's secondhand VHS player all to myself.

I knew what cruising was, and I knew the names of a few parts of Madrid where it happened. I was aware of bathhouses and porn theaters, and I knew how they worked. I had also heard of clandestine gay bars; they'd been around until very recently, places where you had to knock on the door so they could decide from inside who would be let in. When I read about those things, it seemed to me that the community had created something beautiful with the shadows they'd been con-demned to. A unique, urgent, self-aware way of being together without hang-ups, a school for bodies without the buried vio-lence that lounged effortlessly under the sun of heterosexuality and among those who'd raised me. I didn't need to read about that violence or learn it from the movies; I had seen it with my own eyes.

The fact that I saw beauty in the way pleasure and the desire to love one another prevailed didn't mean life should always be lived like that, in the dark, avoiding the sunlight, fearing it be-cause beneath it waited the monsters. I felt happy to be able to give Antonio, and perhaps other people having a coffee there, an image of hope. It was strange to feel so much fear, see life as so dark, see yourself as so disfigured, and at the same time, be aware that, seen through the right lens, I myself, gripping my first lover's hand, was the promise of a brighter future.

FAMILY

t was getting late, and the place was starting to fill up. Antonio moved perkily through the space; everything in his body language emphasized that the café was his home. His gestures and his hoarse voice contained a welcoming and poignant femininity. Watching him, I understood that I would always trust swishy men and that, in the future, I would even love a few. Antonio smiled at all the customers and chatted with everyone who came in the door, whether he already knew them or it was their first time at the Figueroa. He was a short, bearded, dark-haired man, with the thick neck and back of a descendant of a long line of men and women who'd worked their fingers to the bone. His thin legs also told the story of the malnutrition endemic to families who had only ever known backbreaking work. He treated people with a natural warmth that made everybody feel at home; he'd softened my stiffness and defused my fear with just a couple of jokes. That afternoon,

I only had eyes, mouth, and hands for Jay, but I wasn't bothered when Antonio interrupted us. In fact, I wished his interruptions were longer, and I was left with a volley of questions stuck in my throat, things I wanted to ask him just so I could hear him speak.

As dusk was falling, we decided it was time to go somewhere else, even though we had no clear destination. We had already occupied the table an unseemly length of time considering how little we'd ordered. We went to the bar to pay and say goodbye to our host.

"You leaving already, schoolkids? You going somewhere else or back home?"

"We're going for a walk," I answered. "We still have some time but don't really know what to do. We're not familiar with this area, so we're just gonna stroll around; that's it."

I realized how relaxed I was, as if in those two or three hours, I'd breathed in new air that had distanced me from my childhood. I was aware that at fourteen, I was too young to be hanging around that scene, but by the time I was old enough, maybe I'd be ready. I felt clear, as if my birth veil had lifted. I had accepted years of longing and cleared away doubts that weighed heavy as a cross, all in one afternoon. When you're so far away from everything and can't touch it, you judge how it will feel based on your own fears and the fears you've learned. I realized that fear affected me in a particular way, stranding me in a perpetual state of immaturity by keeping me at arm's length from all significant experience. This wasn't about doing things I wasn't old enough to be doing yet, but about getting a sense that another life was possible, a life beyond terror, stagnation, and crying alone. As it turned out, I'd learned in those few hours in the Figueroa with Jay, and in part thanks to Antonio, that there was a world outside in which I stood a chance. I didn't know what the folks in that café would think about women like me—I figured they'd probably met a few—but I sensed that if there was a possibility of flinging myself into the void of freedom and landing on fresh, soft grass, it was among people like those, just from the glimpse of them I'd seen in the time it takes to drink a coffee and kiss until my lips were numb.

"Wait, let me give you some condoms." He said "condoms" in an even tone; he could've been saying "some perfectly ripe figs." I tried to maintain my composure at the word. My life in the closet and my adolescence brought about those contradictory feelings. I knew the exact width of Jay's hips, and I could trace them in the air with my hands perfectly, but I was shocked by the mere mention of condoms.

"This guy," said Antonio, looking at Jay, "has used them before, but you haven't, am I right?"

"I know what they are, and I've seen some on the ground near where my dad works. There's a lot that fills up with couples at night who park there to fuck. I think my brother carries some in his wallet. I don't go near them. I've never used one. I don't need them."

"Okay. Well, you do need them; get this guy to show you how to put one on, and make him wear one every time he's with you. Nothing ever happens until it does."

"And *you*, maricón," he addressed Jay, tapping him on the chest with the back of his hand. "You should *always* wear one; be careful. Care-ful." He communicated with Jay in the age-old Spanish tradition of speaking very slowly and loudly to for-eigners. Antonio wasn't a polyglot, but he got his point across clearly, and in fact, Jay understood Spanish much better than he spoke it. His inability to converse fluently gave the impres-sion that he was much more lost than he really was; actually he grasped almost everything right off the bat.

I thanked him, grabbed the strip of condoms, and slipped it into a chest pocket of my jean jacket. Before we turned to leave, I wanted to ask about something that'd been nagging at me since we'd come in. I was always fixated on having spaces scoped out. My experience as trans and queer forced me to keep an obsessively close eye on any room I set foot in. As soon as I entered, I would take in the layout of the furniture, any pic-tures on the walls, possible entrances and exits, and windows. Above all else, I made sure to memorize, interpret, and record every human face inside, along with their expressions and their gazes when laughing, serious, or surprised. That feeling of control helped me to manage the closet, and with all those factors, I could calculate fairly precisely how careful I had to be about my gestures, words, and looks. The result was almost always extreme caution; there was very rarely any hint of queerness in the spaces that would drop the alert level to moderate. The Figueroa was a fantabulous new experience of relaxation, probably the first in my entire life, since my meetings with Jay were always under threat of being caught and punished. Not even my cross-dressing sessions in the bathroom escaped that logic; the only thing protecting me from catastrophe was a fragile lock and an appropriate response from the other side of the door.

The first thing I'd noticed when I'd entered the Figueroa was a wall behind the bar that wasn't filled with shelves of bottles. It was an unobstructed space painted dark green, where several photographic portraits hung in identical frames.

"Hey, Antonio, before we go, can I ask you something?"

"Sure, girl, give me a minute. I have two tables I need to get to, and then I'll be back."

He returned quickly. He was able to do his job speedily without rushing, moving between the tables with the joy of an urban, indoor Bacchus. He was agile, exuding generosity with every step, and still had the perfect sprinkle of mischief and malice you'd expect of the god of wine, banquets, and pleasure.

"Go on, sweetie, what's on your mind?"

"Who are those people in the photos? I've been looking at

them all afternoon, and I'm so curious. I suppose they're regulars or something like that. . . . I was thinking that I'd like to bring you a photo of us, so we could be here forever. That's probably silly of me."

Imagining myself with Jay, my first lover, adorning the walls of the first place I could grab him by the hands in front of other people seemed so lovely to me. Photos on walls are important. Madonna was always on my bedroom walls because there were moments in my life when she was the only one there for me, like a virgin of warped lives I could tell my sorrows to and beg for protection. The clippings of Bowie, Boy George, and Pete Burns that I had taped to my headboard allowed me to fantasize about change and hope for the beauty one longs for from a false masculinity before finally abandoning it. The poster of Siouxsie on the back of my bedroom door encouraged me to be less compassionate—more selfish, dark, and dangerous. Morrissey, who also watched over my sleep from that door, was Marcabru, and I, Eleanor of Aquitaine; he sang my yearnings and my impossible loves. I loved him with the distance ladies projected on troubadours. He made me live other lives; he helped me escape. George Michael and Dave Gahan shared a reversible poster on the wall that faced me as I went to sleep. They both drove me wild with desire and foretold that someday, flesh against flesh would cure some of my wounds and my fears. Every night, I went to sleep looking at the faces of that book of brazen saints in vinyl and makeup, and I prayed to them from a life that only grew narrower and narrower. They were there, I swear, like the angels in Botticelli's paintings, ruling from clouds that couldn't sustain me but which promised me different worlds.

"All of those folks are gone, sweetheart."

My question had changed Antonio's expression. His face dimmed while remaining sweet. More than a shadow, it was longing that darkened his gaze. A crystalline distance, a sad and lovely melody that you could only hear if you listened very intently.

"They were my friends; this one here, my boyfriend, look, poor thing, he was so ugly and so good." He kissed his fingertips and then stroked the smiling mouth of the man in the photograph. "They were the family I formed when I arrived in Madrid twenty-five years ago."

We stood a couple of feet from the wall, and I wouldn't say that the café fell silent, but the volume did drop significantly. The atmosphere changed in seconds. All the serenity and joy that seemed to travel with the swirls of smoke from table to table transformed into something invisible, with the consistency of prayers and good memories that fade over time, a handful of sand that, no matter how tight we grip it, slips through our fingers. Many of the customers were looking at the wall; some looked at us, and others looked with glassy eyes out into nowhere, perhaps at their own private wall of photos.

Antonio continued. "This here is Celestino, my Celes." His hand was still on the same framed photo. "We were in Torremolinos. I took this shot; we were having a fucking amazing time that summer. A civil guard patrol caught us fooling around on the side of the road in the Mijas mountains, and Celestino convinced them he was giving me an asthma massage. He was as charming as he was ugly, and what a way with words."

He pointed to another photo. It was a portrait in black and white of someone wearing a lot of makeup and posing theatrically. It was a lovely snapshot, like a showgirl captured by Man Ray.

"This one here is Sarita; her name was Bernardo, but she would get really mad if we called her that. She said that sounded like the name of some custard-loving priest. They kicked her out of the Colmenar Viejo barracks for imitating Sara Montiel during the nightly guard watches they had to do in the army. There my Sarita would start singing "La violetera" in a uniform jacket and panties, in full makeup. That took guts. What a pair of ovaries she had."

I was fascinated by the photo of Sarita; perhaps it held the answer to my lingering question of whether this would be a welcoming place for me when the moment came. I stared at her with the same urgency that compelled me to stare at Margarita when I was smaller, but without a hint of repulsion. I felt the hands of the company of ghosts on my shoulders, comforting me. If only Sarita were there listening to Antonio talk about her so lovingly. If only I could have some time to talk to her, ask her questions, from a girl who wore makeup in secret to a girl who wore makeup in front of the entire San Pedro Logistic Support Brigade at the Colmenar Viejo headquarters.

"I'm sorry, Antonio. I didn't mean to make you sad; I shouldn't have asked."

"Oh no, sweetheart, these people were my whole world, and I lost them along the way, but they've never really left. I love talking about them; I love when people ask about them. I miss them so much, but I have them here, in my little café, watching over me from the wall and cheering me on. You know those elderly widows who get up every morning and kiss photos of their dead husbands and prayer cards of Saint Anthony of Padua? Well, I do the same thing but with this pack of gorgeous faggots. My family. I come in here, and it's the first thing I do: I say good morning to them, kiss the ones who deserve it, and then get to work. You can imagine what happened to most of them; that's why I hand out condoms to baby gays like I'm Santa Claus. I can get very overbearing, like a mom from La Mancha, and, believe me, I know it's weird for a stranger to tell you what you should be doing with your own equipment . . . but, girrrrl, I prefer you come back someday in the flesh and read me to filth over coffees than seeing you frozen into a photo forevermore."

I realized that I was squeezing Jay's hand very tightly. I've always been solemn by nature, and memorials and altars have always had an impact on me. Again the idea that everything beautiful ends up overcome by darkness coalesced in my mind. It wasn't Antonio's fault; he'd told us the story of that wall with much affection and very little gravity, but the certainty that one day I would lose everything I cared about had become recurrent. I was the queen of self-fulfilling prophecies.

"I don't want you to think of that wall as a horror show," continued Antonio. "Or to go home all sad and hide under the bed. I'm looking at your faces, and it's like we just had a séance, maricones. These are photos of my family, the one I chose, just like the family you'll have someday and that's probably already out there looking for you. Being like us is fabulous. The fact that you asked me about them means that you're needing them. Pay attention; your family will show up when you least expect it—right here, for example. I'll stop there; I'm getting more annoying than the clock in *Beauty and the Beast*."

"Can I give you a hug?" I asked, trying in vain not to cry.

"Come on, baby girl, bring it in." He hugged me tightly and for a good long while; I left the front of his shirt wet with tears that were no longer those of a little girl.

When it was Jay's turn to say goodbye, they had a brief whispered exchange, and when they pulled apart, I saw Antonio give him a set of keys with some directions he hastily scribbled onto a napkin. Then Jay threw himself into his arms and rested his head on Antonio's shoulder with an almost childlike sweetness. Beneath Jay's charming mischievousness was a child who needed attachments, only emerging for a few seconds after fucking or in moments of uncontrollable emotion, which were few and far between. That image of Jay letting himself be almost rocked by Antonio was a lightning bolt of faith and tragic beauty to my eyes. I couldn't help seeing a descension in it, an apostle caring for Jesus's rigid body.

PER SEMPRE

Antonio's house was small and poorly lit. The front door led directly into a well-laid-out living room, especially considering its size. He kept it uncluttered. Beside an enormous French window that yawned from the ceiling to the floor, he'd placed a little coffee table and two metal chairs that didn't take up much space but added life to the room. You could imagine Antonio breakfasting in silence there, seated and gazing out the window.

Apart from a two-seater sofa up against the wall opposite the large window and a couple of narrow but solid and full bookshelves that filled another part of the wall, there was nothing else.

I must've read too many books by Truman Capote, because I was expecting Antonio's house to be filled with tchotchkes and textures, something befitting a mature maricón. I wasn't expecting that tidy austerity; his taste was undeniably good, but rather on the minimalist side.

I didn't ask Jay, and I didn't want to know what sort of agreement had brought us that privacy. I'm not saying that it seemed shady; it was probably just a thoughtful favor from Antonio because he thought we were sweet. He would know better than anyone about those pilgrimages to nowhere that dates could turn into when they were between fags, dykes, and other inhabitants of our forest. Whatever the reason, I was fine with it.

We started kissing as soon as we got inside, leaning against the door; we kissed on our way to the bedroom, which was at the end of a hallway so short, it was hardly worthy of the designation.

"Give me a moment, Jay."

We'd had our moments before; I had no lingering apprehension. I wasn't nervous, and I didn't need to prepare. I needed him bad, and I needed him as soon as possible. We had gotten used to searching for the most hidden corners of the most remote parks we knew, to get a bit of pleasure. Sometimes we would sneak into less risky places, like closed schoolyards, making sure there was no custodian. There were a few entryways blessed by our fleeting encounters even though that scared me, so we didn't often take the risk of making love in stairwells.

I knew how Jay smelled, how he tasted, and how he moved. But he didn't know everything he should've known about me. I had never been completely naked with him, and I thought that the first time I was going to have real privacy and safety with someone who felt the same way about me, with someone I liked so much and didn't fear at all, I wasn't going to do it hog-tied by the unsaid and the unrevealed.

"Of course, of course, what's going on, you is nervous? Antonio no come nor nobody. I don't mind being late; I want to be with you and promise you you not late home."

It was a shame he wasn't more fluent; I knew he wanted to tell me something more, make me feel more secure. He didn't know it, but he'd already accomplished that with his tone, his gestures, and his gaze. Jay was pure joy, and sometimes he went too fast, but he took care of me and never put me in an uncomfortable situation. The opposite, in fact. With him, everything was easy. His difficulties with conversing fluently and my bastard high-school English made me sadder for him than for me. In his native English, he must've sounded like a prince.

"No, I'm not nervous, really. I just want to talk to you about something important."

I hated how keeping secrets compelled me to such solemnity. Everything that had to do with my identity, when I was rehearsing possibilities of explaining it, sounded like a confession, of a crime or some unforgivable sin. Having grown up with the language of guilt disseminated from every corner as the only way to refer to trans lives was disheartening. Discovering one's self should be cause for celebration; the public release from a suffo-cating space should be met with hugs and relief. But how can you even imagine something you've never seen or even sensed? Who'd ever heard of a fag or dyke being congratulated by their parents and friends for being who they were, or a bisexual being treated any way other than pathological and dirty or just not taken seriously because there's no such thing as bisexuality, or a cross-dresser walking down the street with proud parents beside them? No conversation about repudiating your gender was ever delivered lightly, which had nothing to do with its importance. It was impossible to conceive of any way of explaining myself that didn't involve dramatically setting the stage with gravity, guilt, and forecasted rejection.

"Let me show you something."

I grabbed my wallet; I was carrying it in the back pocket of the pants I still hadn't taken off. I ripped open the Velcro, pulled my metro card out of its compartment, and flipped it over. On the back of the document was a collage of photos of Madonna and Lily Munster, and below that, hidden, a single cutout image that no one could see. I extracted it carefully and gave it to Jay.

"Do you know who that is?" I asked him. By that point, I was trembling a little bit.

"I don't know. Who?" he asked, with true curiosity and no pressure.

He had adapted his stance to express closeness, not desire. I immediately felt his respect for my need to talk, and he opened himself up completely to take in what I had to tell him.

"It's Alessandra Di Sanzo, the star of an Italian film from two or three years back that I saw recently; it's called *Forever Mary*. The original title is *Mery per sempre*. She is transsexual."

"I thunked she was a girl."

He held my gaze intently as he said that. I think in that moment, he understood everything and didn't need much more. But this conversation was starting to be more for me than for him. I was settling my scores with the spoken word, with speaking out loud, with naming myself for the first fucking time in my life.

"Thought. You say 'thought,' not 'thunked.' And she is a girl."

"Thought."

"That's it, thought. In the movie, her character starts out as a boy who sells his body, dressed as a girl . . . a whore, a hooker. She ends up in jail because of a john, and there she meets a teacher. . . . Well, that's not important. She's a boy who wants to be a girl and . . ."

Jay smiled because that was his natural default, but he was serious, and he was clearly intent on understanding each and every word I was telling him.

"Help me, Mery!" I would often entrust myself to the magazine clippings and posters that I treasured as if they were images of saints that watched over me. "She, he, she tells in the movie how she knows she will never have a normal life, that she'll never have anyone waiting at home for her, that she won't have children, things like that. In Italian, she says, '*Io non sono né carne né pesce, io sono Mery, Mery per sempre.*'" I have never been able to say that sentence out loud without crying. I couldn't help it then in that shadowy bedroom beside Jay. "I'm neither fish nor fowl, Jay." I took his face in my hands and brought it close to mine. "I wish I could name myself aloud, a name that fits me, but I have none. It scares me to be like this, and I've tried to avoid it. I never show my body because it is turning into a labyrinth of rotting flesh that I don't know how to escape. I work very hard to conform to what's expected of me; I stop my dreams by slapping myself. You can't imagine what it's like to smack yourself at dawn because you wake up in the middle of a dream where all you're doing is dancing surrounded by stars and looking at yourself in a magic mirror that reflects back a marvelous image. I can fool others, and I do it very well. But this. Is. Still. Here." I let go of his face, and I sunk the fingernails on both hands into his chest as I said it. "And it's not going anywhere. It never leaves me. I'm like my neighbor Margarita; I'm like Sarita, Antonio's friend; I'm like Mery, like Mery most of all. I live between two worlds with nobody waiting at home for me in either one. But I'm not as brave as they were, Jay. I'm going to be this all my life: Alejandro, Álex, Álex *per sempre*. And no one can save me."

Jay was now crying softly with me, his breathing and expression unchanged. He had understood nothing, yet he'd understood everything. My first intention with that confession was to level with my first love and to show up to what would be our only private encounter, with the nakedness owed a real lover. As it progressed, it ceased to be something I was offering to him and became something I had to say to myself, out loud. I said what I had to say, aware that Jay would get lost in words and sentences too complex for his level of Spanish; I trusted that my eyes and my trembling would fill in the blanks. Jay let tears slide down his cheeks, one after the other, crying in silence. I had pulled away from him and sat up in the bed to speak. Once I had, everything was loneliness, cold, and a bitter relief, similar to the feeling of just having vomited with the inevitable bad taste left in your mouth.

"Come to side." He patted the mattress with his palm to invite me to draw closer. "I cannot save, not wait home nor nothing. Not life whole. Whole life." He wrenched the words out as if grabbing clumps of mud. "But tonight, I can." He opened his arms and welcomed me into them. I trusted him, but I'd never expected to ever experience a moment like that. He kissed me on the cheek once, twice, three times, making his way towards my ear. When it was in his reach, he caressed it with his lips and whispered, "I will never call you Álex again. To me, if want, I call you Sempre. Just Sempre."

What happened after that made up for lost time, taking out a loan that at some point in the future I'd be asked to pay back in spades. Damn time, it was always being wrenched away from women like me. Time to be girls; time to be teenagers; time for awkward loves; time for foolish crying; time to make girlfriends, fight with them, and make up immediately; time to dance like maniacs; uninterrupted time to learn how to be women. We're allowed none of that growing up, or only in fits and starts; we have to rob from fate and rush anxiously, like drinking from wells in the middle of the desert, knowing that we'll be dying of thirst before we find the next one.

That evening, as dusk bloomed into night, being with Jay was like walking barefoot on fresh grass, without seriousness, without panic, without snarled dramas I had to disentangle in order to feel alive. Having him inside me and hearing him laugh, because he would laugh while fucking, was wanting to die and halt everything because nothing that life had in store for me would ever be better than that. He did it all and did it all well, or exactly the way I needed it. Being a man, being a woman, not being either of those two things, is something that can't be experienced or constructed alone. My woman's body needed to provoke desire on its own terms, needed to be defined by eager hands, to move freely as if dancing, and to trigger the appropriate responses. That was being a teenager for the first time with no objections, no shadows on the wall, no harsh voices shouting humiliations into my ear. I discovered that, although elusive and fleeting, gender euphoria did exist, and it was bursting out everywhere from inside me. In that bedroom, during that encounter, I didn't want to be anyone else but me, for the first time in my life.

SELF-FULFILLED
PROPHECY

One knows she loves unselfconsciously when she stops fearing the gestures that give her away as a lover. And if she still fears them, then she at least lowers her guard, allowing herself a wider range of motions. That, in those shameful years, taught us both a definitive lesson about first-rate and second-rate lives. Jay usually put on his karate uniform in front of the mirror, with the confidence of someone who adored his body. I put on mine seated on a bench without ever removing my undershirt. We'd arrived early to the gym; it was a habit we'd adopted so we could change alone together. We were very careful with what our bodies did beneath that damp ceiling gnawed by black mold. We never touched each other and merely looked at each other complicitly. But when you're in love, or think you're in love, and you've only been on this earth for fourteen years—most of which had been spent erecting defenses that were incredibly difficult to maintain—sooner rather than later, you'll make a mistake, the kind that's very costly to lives like ours. The locker room was silent, and its door creaked when it was opened, in a quite noisy and unpleasant announcement of anyone coming in. I approached Jay from behind and kissed him on the base of his neck, a quick kiss, the kind that makes no noise. He tilted his head to one side and back, resting it on mine. We hadn't realized when we came in that the door didn't creak. The owner, the master, who kept the place a pigsty to give it an air of austerity, had decided it was a good day to oil the hinges. All we heard was a "yuck." I didn't dare look; I closed my eyes and remained petrified as if someone had stolen my clothes and illuminated me with a spotlight. The ghosts that accompany me tried to cover my shame, but they were unable to with their misty bodies. Soon, I would be another story like theirs.

"Being like us is fabulous." Antonio's voice, in front of his wall of the happy dead, faded in the ditch my mind had become. No, it wasn't. No, it wasn't going to be. I would've liked to defend our beauty with lovely words; I would've liked to know how to use pride, rage, and self-love. How can you wield sentiments you've never fully believed in, how if every time people talk about you and your kind, they invoke malignancy? Everything that was beautiful and had ever touched us fell into the ditch, while all my hands could do was tremble. Away from Jay's sculpting hands, I again became an undesirable, incapable of putting up a fight, someone who vested others with the power to destroy my life with a mere look. I opened my eyes. I was in front of the mirror; Jay had gone back to the bench near the locker to finish getting ready for class as if nothing had happened. The mirror reflected back to me Margarita's gaze, her narrow world, her limits, and her warnings.

The snitch who set into motion the corrective machinery—a trivial monitor who poured all his inability to lead a functional, real life into that martial arts pantomime, the "right hand" of the master, a rube with authority over just 215 square feet— was looking where he shouldn't have been, when he shouldn't have been, and, with what he saw or thought he saw, he had enough to assert his parcel of power. He made sure that Jay's family knew what had happened; from their reaction, he probably turned our gesture of tenderness into a story of saliva and animal sodomy. He was the type of person who needed to see others' pleasure and love as disgusting acts because both were off-limits to him. He didn't say anything to my family. He tried to seek out a certain complicity with me thanks to the *huge favor* he thought he'd done for me by not telling my parents about Jay and banishing the temptation of his sacred body. When I rejected that complicity, the favor turned into an ace up his sleeve for blackmail and control.

Just as I found him, I lost him. A locker-room beginning and a locker-room end. Since that night at Antonio's house, we'd seen each other only a few times, following the usual protocol: short encounters, discretion, and hardly any words. As Jay had promised, he never called me anything but Sempre, even with others around, including at the gym. I can't even establish when was the last time we were in each other's arms. From one day to the next, Jay disappeared, and snakes coiled in my stomach as I hypothesized the consequences he might have faced. Instead of directing all my scorn and all the evil eye I could muster at the person responsible for that pain, someone who interloped in our lives because he wanted to and because he could, I devoted myself to reviewing each and every possible misstep. Again the lessons of guilt and deflection became omnipresent in my mind. Everything in our rearing was warnings, alerts, and bad omens whose only purpose was to throw an "I told you so" into our faces. Nobody should grow up thinking that, no matter what they do, they'll end up making a fatal mistake. And there I was, making my heart sacred through stabbings and fires at the stake, with no way out, one step back for every step forward, closing my closet from the inside, slapping myself in the middle of the night, and asking for help from the chorus of the dead who waited by the corners of my bed, pale, translucent, and sad.

Silence and uncertainty coiled in my throat, which grew more constrained every passing day. I barely finished the school year.

I had no way to get in touch with him. I knew his address, but they had sent him away, and we had no friends in common who could help me. I thought about turning to Antonio; I could've used some adult recourse but didn't dare go back there alone. Every day that passed, I shut down a little more, and it wasn't a question of heartbreak, or not just that. It wasn't about a teenage broken heart treading water through petty drama. I had abruptly matured enough to know how to read the situation in all its complexity. There were many factors in play: my shame, my concern for his safety, and my feeling of impotence at never being able to win. My life, the relationships with my loved ones, my public image, depended on the whim of some abominable guy puffed up on self-importance. I considered offering him anything he wanted for his silence; I was sure he would've accepted a couple of blow jobs initially, but eventually he would've demanded more. I opted to accept the uncertainty of his discretion rather than end up catering to the needs of a piece of shit who, under normal circumstances, I wouldn't have gone anywhere near.

With an open rift in my mental health that would anticipate the debacle and isolation of later years, I let the months pass. Anguish became more self-contempt, fear remained fear, pain transformed into a spectral fog that brought me back down to the depths from which I could see life but, once again, couldn't touch it.

My brilliant grades were over, the kindly face of my closet was over, survival meant letting it all go. My family was too busy working their fingers to the bone to notice my decline. When it became very obvious, it was already too late to intervene; it had become my skin.

Sometimes I saw Margarita around the neighborhood. She was much worse for wear since her mother's death; she never recovered that spark of tranny power that I had seen, with her high bun, pink cheeks, and shiny brown lips. I was tempted to talk to her several times; I think she would've understood me or at least listened lovingly. But the gulf that had opened up between me and the world could not be bridged. I was just another bitter fag, another transsexual defeated too soon, another tragic transvestite, another unimportant story that no one loved or wanted to help. Fodder for the metro tracks. That year was the first time I seriously thought about grinding my flesh up beneath iron wheels.

Jay gradually faded from my memory, taking on the timbre of things that never existed. His memory survived inside me, but he did not. It was strange to lose the traces of his touch, his aroma, and his voice, and at the same time, have him lodged in some part of my mind that was too easy for me to access. Fuck, it had only been eight or nine dates.

The guy who broke us up never exposed me; I liked to think that decision had something to do with a modicum of shame on his part. As for me, the lesson had been more than learned. If I wanted to have something resembling a life, it had to be beyond the surveillance of normalcy, hidden, minimizing the possibility of commonplace corrective violence. The rest of the time, I decided to go with the flow until something better happened or until I got tired of it. Lying, acting, distrusting, and keeping myself safe in the gloomy castle of my loneliness.

All I had left was the hope that Jay was remaking his life wherever he was. I always knew that our devotion to each other was unbalanced, and I never believed he was head over heels in love with me; that would've been in bad taste. Imagining him overcoming Lieutenant Nichols's hurdles and, once the unpleasant incident had blown over in his family, returning to his adventures, relieved an important part of my poisoned thinking loops. Jay was a sensual and elusive spirit; he was Bagoas, the Persian dancer, capable of surviving Alexander the Great himself. Of course he would survive me.

NOCTURNE

arrived punctually to the five-cornered wasteland. I was wearing a formfitting water dress, and my wings were only half unfurled as befitted the hour of night, when the spheres were not yet singing but did reveal themselves. It was my first waxing gibbous in Leo and the sixth meeting with other creatures of the forest in the summer of Antares. My obsidian heels were hurting because I wasn't used to wearing them, but as soon as my wings unfurled and I managed to relieve the load off my feet, that discomfort disappeared, and I could flaunt them with the nimbleness demanded of me.

Soon the space filled, and we joined others, wings with horns, backbones with cleft hooves, skins of flame layered with moss. As soon as the hunchbacked queen debuted, she poured her light into our mouths, and we surrendered, as one should, our eternal souls to start the dance. An almost bitter taste sloshed over my tongue, and suddenly everything became bodies responding to the moon's lunacy, to the music of the spheres, to pain and pleasure and each and every step between one and the other. I wanted to approach the void, to look into the face of the great sorceress without going blind, but the internal currents of the dance swaying to the rattle of the sistrum and the ensuing tectonic flesh games jostled me involuntarily left and right. To even glimpse the source, entire lives had to take part in the dance. I stopped trying and closed my wings, only to return to the obsidian pain and entrust myself to the stabs of some dragon who smelled fresh meat that night. I lost myself in the ritual until a jolt pulled me from him. A voice behind me, the voice of a man who had his hand on my right shoulder, asked if I was okay. He slowly undid our union. I turned around, kissed him very unhurriedly and deeply, with the cadence of abandon and the tired passion of gratitude; he tasted of dragon. I didn't say anything to him or touch him again. I left that hot darkness and entered the part of the place that was illuminated. I didn't know if I should look for the bathroom to drink some water—I was dying of thirst—or look for the exit. I stood for a moment in the middle of that space, somewhat less packed than the one I'd left behind, settling into a cold sludge that presaged a bad break of day. I asked for the time with a gesture, tapping my fingers on the wrist of an androgynous and incredibly sad Hermes who was in a full-body embrace of a loudspeaker booming "Better Things" by Massive Attack. He looked into my eyes and said nothing; he just moved his head very slowly, trying and failing to follow the beat, as if he were hearing a different rhythm inside him. His distance made me horny, and I considered dragging him into the darkness and devouring him, but my heartburn reminded me that I was tied down by this damn earth and needed to rest. Before leaving, I looked back at him; perhaps we'd been expelled from the same dance, and he hadn't managed to look into the face of the hunchbacked queen, either.

It was almost daybreak when I walked down the Gran Vía towards Cibeles; the temptation to catch the night bus never won out over my impulse to walk, even when I was parched, exhausted, and my entrails were throbbing. At a good clip, my neighborhood was an hour and a half from the center of Madrid. Walking, like running, was a way to feel that I wasn't immobilized by the fiery orbit of the world, that life wasn't a maelstrom impossible to weather through. Walking was moving, doing something, offering some resistance to a pliancy that was eating me alive.

I usually waited to get back to my hood to change, but my feet couldn't take anymore. I was wearing very tight fake vinyl pants; simple black stilettos; and a cropped Nirvana T-shirt that I'd bought at a flea market in Alfaz del Pi a couple of summers before. I dressed with enough femininity to appease my impulses for a few more days but with enough ambiguity to be able to pass off as a dark fairy if need be.

At some point past where Alcalá turns into O'Donnell, on the sidewalk that runs along Retiro Park, I sat down on a bench to change my footwear. I was carrying black sneakers in my backpack alongside a change of clothes I would wear to arrive home. I was overcome by waves of nausea; the same thing happened every time I took ecstasy, but I had already learned that vomiting in those circumstances, instead of relieving my discomfort, just made it worse. I was dehydrated and on an empty stomach, and the only thing I could bring up was a liquid that tasted of misery.

While I was tying my shoelaces, a man stopped quite close in front of me, wearing a plastic poncho like Robin Williams in *The Fisher King*. His pants were down, and he was massaging an unresponsive cock he seemed to be trying to bring back to life. I figured the poor devil was harboring the hope that my presence would aid his miracle resuscitation, but God almost never shows up when one hopes, because He is darkness. He had to create light, shouting into the abyss, in order to see something more than Himself and His shadows. I attended that gloomy man's clumsy maneuvers with an indifferent gaze; at some point, he seemed to be enjoying my attention very much, but he couldn't muster more than a half-mast. Pasolini would have relished that like a kid on Christmas morning. Without looking away, I started to remove my makeup with the wet wipes I always carried. It wasn't easy; I wore a generous amount to conceal coarse, thick facial hair that had spread over my face like an infection. I rubbed so hard, it hurt. It took a lot of wipes to get my face more or less clean. The lipstick came off easily but left a red trail around my mouth that looked like a rash; the eye shadow also gave way quickly, but the eyeliner and mascara were quite resistant. I always arrived home with some traces of black on my eyes, but I didn't care. My alibi was Christian Death, Lacrimosa, and my early conversion to goth, which was an accepted and lovely way to cross-dress in public, eliciting somewhat less violent responses than when doing it just out of need or for glory.

When the bluish shadow of a beard began to emerge on my face, the fisher king recalled his bait immediately. "What? A faggot!" he said, with more disappointment than anger, and he took his leave, hoisting up his pants clumsily, walking like a leprechaun avoiding cow patties.

Yes, that was one of those nights when I needed to be a faggot or whatever it was. Those nights were my fragments of life on my own terms, my walks in search of some type of communion or oblivion that rescued me from ordinary life under the sun. I had resigned myself to living that way; I'd surrendered to the battering tides, letting their comings and goings do with me what they would. But on those very few nights, I journeyed through my body's possibilities in the worst way, roughly calling out the woman I was and was not.

I was entering adulthood without any hope. During my adolescence, after the bad ending to my first love story, I became aware of a reality I could not overcome: I lied not to suffer. Then a divided road opened up before me. I'd traveled along some of its paths as a child, and it ended up being the only one available to me. I could have fought differently, been more brave, but I wasn't; the moment in my life when I was gathering enough bravery, enough pride, and enough beauty to be able to vindicate myself as a proud young woman, had culminated in blackmail and a separation that felt more like a kidnapping. My inability to react or resist had sent me back into the realm of childhood fears, of an immaturity that preferred a life of bathrooms and locks, projecting normalcy, overcompensating a masculinity that manifested as tragedy and farce.

I reached my parents' home around seven thirty in the morning, finished changing my clothes right before going up, already in the building, on a landing where I knew a deaf neighbor lived alone. Doing that at eighteen was humiliating, but humiliation usually goes hand in hand with depression. I stopped caring that I looked like a total idiot. The apartment was near silent; I could hear a shower running and a transistor radio that my mother carried around everywhere as she worked inside and outside the house. She woke up with the radio and went to sleep with it playing under her pillow. It was her weekend shower schedule, an hour or two later than on weekdays. My father had already left for work; in those days, he had the Saturday shift. There were no deliveries, which is what he usually did, supplying clients with their products, but there was always work overhauling the printers, die cutters, and paper cutters, or tidying up the warehouse. I peeked into the bathroom where my mother was showering to let her know I'd arrived.

"Son, I was just about to call the police to go looking for you or file a missing person's. The sun's already up." From inside the shower, her voice was muffled by the stream of water. She was angry but used to it. "Go on, get some rest."

I responded with a smile she couldn't see and went to bed. That kind of scolding was her way of loving me, and that's how I took it, like a Marian blessing. I placed the clothes I'd worn into an opaque plastic bag, similar to a garbage bag but with handles. I pressed it as flat as I could, squeezing out all the air and knotting it before I put it up on the top shelf of my closet, where I kept old books and posters and other stuff destined to live out their days in some confined space or in an attic. I piled the bag on top of two others with more hidden clothes, and I organized the shelf so that it looked like entropy continued doing its job.

I put on an old T-shirt to get into bed. Sleeping in the nude was impossible; when I was aware of the shapes of my body, of how they lay on the mattress, brushing freely against the sheets, or how they relaxed and distributed the tension and weight, I was incapable of calming down. Once I was dressed, after those nights of dragon-men and dancing, there was no anxiety that could hinder my sleep, and I would quickly cross the threshold into the slumberer's great beyond. But before I did, I dedicated a drunken prayer to my family of ghosts and fell asleep.

NO BIG DEAL

lived in fear of the judgment of an invisible god who chan-
neled himself in the gazes surrounding me, a sacred hunter
spirit that leapt from body to body and swirled around me
like a vulture waiting for a wounded animal to give up the ghost.
He knew why I had started to fake my behavior, to masculinize
it, when I was a girl. He remembered the adult words and atti-
tudes that had become etched into my inner game room and
had burned it down. As I grew up, my life inescapably diverged,
like tectonic plates separating; there was no way to hold on to
the edges and fuse them into some uninterrupted existence. I
was convinced that every attempt to vindicate myself as the girl,
teenager, and woman that I was would be followed by some
unbearable corrective backlash.

My experiences after Jay hadn't helped dissipate that fear;
the correctives were constant, daily, in casual conversations
I overheard, in jokes, in films, in the brutal rejection of the

teenage world, in everything. I remember a crowded family birthday function in which an uncle of mine, his mouth full of cake, put forth to the men a hypothetical of choosing between "getting fucked up the ass or shot dead," like someone choosing between ice-cream flavors, thinking it was a pertinent, kind question that would enliven the afternoon. Without exception, all my male family members chose the bullet, with much laughter and ease, participating in a joke of no importance. But they chose the bullet. The women didn't lend their complicity; we all felt contempt like that blowing up in our faces occasionally, that disdain for someone who was penetrated being understood as feminine or weak, implying that it was better to die than to be at all womanlike. They could reject that as a group, let the men know they thought they were clowns and their questions, shitty. They were still being treated with contempt, but they had some sisterhood on their side. I had to choke down the humiliation in isolation, as a woman who had no one to share such atrocities with, as a man who had strayed from the path, and as someone who sometimes needed to take it up the ass in order to feel like she was alive.

Faking masculinity, being the tough guy my mother was proud to have given birth to, avoiding the hunter god, I had safeguarded myself from cruelties that, when I saw them inflicted on others, I knew I could not have endured. It was an act of supreme cowardice that was perfected with practice, a form of self-defense that I experienced as what it was: a betrayal of my ghosts. If it was true that pride was possible for people like us, I was undeserving of it. Acting like a man to survive was a privilege, and my awareness of this gnawed at my conscience to the point of physical pain. I started to have migraines that never left me in peace; I was eaten up by muscle spasms and incapable of relaxing. My use of masculine privilege demanded a penance: those nights as a nymph, offering myself to the dragon-men, all to inhabit a body that did not repulse me. But I became obsessed with purging those late nights when dawn broke. Fear and claustrophobia governed my life in the daylight, forcing me to compose a corpse I could leave on the shore for all to see, at the mercy of the diurnal tides. The sun itself whispered in my ear every morning: "Keep digging your grave, you lying bitch, keep digging."

That triumphantly patriarchal sun forced me not only to masculinize myself, but to desensitize myself. I copied my father's way of eating, that of a man who'd known hunger and wasted no time with manners; I perfected his habit of taking big bites, looming slightly over his food, like a predator, his prey. From my brother, I borrowed his hypermasculine body language; he was always an attractive guy the girls really liked and the men admired. I devised my own version, somewhat more austere, with a smaller array of gestures. I stole my way of sitting down and standing up from my Uncle Jacinto, an enormous stonemason with a short fuse. He collapsed onto chairs and rose quickly, like a gorilla responding to provocation. With the school friends I tried to hold on to, more for a shield than genuine connection, part of the same theater of death, I composed the rest of my cadaver.

But there was no hope, and when a sliver appeared, it was soon snuffed out by an excessive reprisal of darkness. Inhabiting a body I didn't know how to occupy, that suffocated me with its narrowness, was already conditioning every step I took, and the passage of that constriction into ordinary life, the paltry world accessible to a woman like me, rendered life meaningless.

With one of those friends of convenience and habit, with whom I managed to establish something close to a bond, the miracle of a confession almost happened. One night when we'd been drinking together and talking calmly, we grazed the deep conversations that as women we hold so easily but that men find so hard. I had taken him into my territory, and he appeared willing to hear difficult things. Until then, he'd always seemed to be the best of my friends—kind, intelligent, understanding, and not prone to cruelty. I suggested we walk home the long way, and he agreed. We were in Malasaña, and on the way back, we had to go through Chueca, which, in just a few years, had already become the flagship gay neighborhood in an institutionally tolerant Madrid. There I was planning to test our friendship and let drop some truths about myself, the easiest ones to accept. More than anything in those days, I needed an alliance, no matter how tepid.

It didn't happen.

"Why don't we go down Génova and cross Colón so we get to Calle de Alcalá sooner?" he suggested, trying to correct the route I had very intentionally proposed.

"I'd rather go through Chueca, past the Cibeles, on Alcalá and O'Donnell. It's nicer; that way, we go along the outside of the Retiro, through Fuente del Berro and Marqués de Corbera. It's practically dead at this time of night, trust me," I replied.

"I'd just rather not go that way, dude."

"What way?"

I didn't know what he was talking about, and I got worried; maybe something had happened to him in one of those parts of the city, something he hadn't told me about, and he was embarrassed or afraid.

"Through the fag neighborhood."

He blurted it out like that, the way he might have said anything else during that evening we'd spent together. Without using a particularly insulting tone. Just the nonchalance with which men denounce what threatens them.

"Dude, what are you saying . . . Don't you know it's called Chueca?"

By that point, inside my head, I could already hear another door of the diurnal world slamming shut; it wasn't even disappointing anymore, but the nip of shame and defeat in my chest was inevitable.

"I just don't like fags. Shit, that's all. No big deal. Let's go a different way."

And no, no big deal, it was never a big deal. Just like at four or five years old, when you already sense that something in you is different, you hear your parents or your neighbors making comments that—you don't know why—hurt you, and you never forget. Words wielded casually that transform into barbed wire that blocks your way and limits your world forever—that was what happened with that false friend. He didn't like fags, the way some people don't like leeks or nougat. A phrase whose calm delivery put another nail in my closet and another stitch in my walking cadaver. My fears and my intuitions, no matter how extreme, weren't wrong. There was no one out there I could place my trust in.

PORKY

woman believes she can put up with anything until she finds herself waving a scarf as she lip-synchs the "Oh, sí, Real Madrid" chant in the nosebleed seats of the Santiago Bernabéu stadium the afternoon after a night in high heels. With pain on the tips of my fingers, on the tip of my tongue, in my ass, in my pride, and suffering advanced symptoms of dehydration. It was such a ridiculous, idiotic situation, unworthy of being classified as tragedy. Rarely have I felt such deep sadness in such a ludicrous atmosphere, so inappropriate for someone dying inside, an atmosphere that, what's more, I had chosen voluntarily.

Of all the absurd rituals I subjected myself to in order to maintain that masquerade, soccer fandom was the most incomprehensible. Letting yourself be carried along by the tide had a price: sometimes it was pure suffering, and other times it was the cost of finding yourself mixed up in asinine rituals, like some medieval theater of cocks and farts. Then all you could do was go with the flow until it was over and later lick the ensuing wounds in private. I started accepting an invite from a friend I'd known since primary school and ended up at the stadium with some regularity. I never felt comfortable amid heterosexual men; I camouflaged best I could and pulled out the thespian I'd been training all my life. That atmosphere was unpleasant and overwhelming. It really bothered me that soccer was the entertainment hopelessly associated with the working class, and it made me sick how journalists would promote saccharine stories of players bringing hope to the humble neighborhoods they'd grown up in. It seemed like another male scheme to impose their entertainment as incontestable mass phenomena. In the period when I frequented that stadium, I saw few women and a lot of boys, the sons of workers, who began by cheering the home team on and ended up with shaved heads and giving the fascist salute.

It was a league match between Madrid and Barcelona, a classic or a derby or whatever they're called. I was feeling terrible: under the weather, my anxiety through the roof. The occasion was unusual in that I wasn't at the stadium only with some neighborhood friends and their buddies, but with my father, too. He didn't show up to games often, but he hadn't wanted to miss such an important match. I felt somewhat better when he came; he didn't mind the crowds, and I liked seeing him happy.

We didn't have many chances to do things together; he always had more things in common with my brother, which was logical. Going to the game or watching it on television with him somewhat relieved my dissociation; it was lovely to be by his side in a context he enjoyed so much. Celebrating goals with a hug was a way to feel close to him, like when I was still a kid. When you pass as a man, you don't have many opportunities to hug your father, even if you want to really badly. That shared space somewhat justified the miserable self-flagellation.

We usually ran into—or we did two or three times—a guy everyone called Porky, one of those people you first sense by those buried instincts that only awaken a handful of times during our lives to alert us to serious danger. It was exactly this survival mechanism that ran through me when I was introduced to Porky. A sleeping danger. He was an acquaintance of someone who lived near a friend of mine. Just another person that fate forced you to socialize with when, under normal circumstances, you would have kept your distance from him. He was very silent after we were introduced, and barely said anything during the metro trip from San Blas to Cuzco. He remained to one side of the group, his hands in the pockets of his green bomber jacket, his head not totally lowered but craning forward, as if trying to aggressively observe. He had the appearance of a person who had the overture to *Carmina Burana* constantly on loop inside his head. He seemed lost in thought but not at peace. He was short, very stocky, with a relatively round face and small, almond-shaped, intensely blue eyes. His nose, clearly the source of his nickname, was so flattened and upturned that it revealed practically vertical nostrils. They introduced him to me as Porky, but I didn't want to call him that. I insisted he tell me his real name or some other option, but he just replied, "Nah, Pork's fine."

All right, Porky it is.

As soon as he set foot in the stadium, that silent guy turned into a vociferous gargoyle who only shut up during halftime to eat a sandwich and drink a beer. He didn't just cheer on his team but insulted the rivals in the worst way possible. Woe was the Black player on Real Madrid who missed a pass, had the ball stolen from them, or made a bad shot at the goal! He shouted out long lists of primates, some of them quite obscure. The sad truth is that no one reacted with the slightest shame to any of it. There wasn't a trace of the wholesome hometown audience that supposedly attended the game with their families. Anyone who'd been to the stadium more than a dozen times knew that such behavior was commonplace; what I wasn't expecting was for the people I'd come with—sure, they weren't role models, but I didn't take them for collaborationists, either—to laugh along with him, only encouraging him to shout even louder. The one sort-of friend I had there seemed to be enjoying it even more than the others. "You're so bad, Porky," he said complicitly, placing a hand on his shoulder after a particularly virulent string of insults. They both laughed.

Madrid won that match, and the crowd went wild; our whole group wanted to go celebrate at the Cibeles Fountain, which for me only had special meaning when it was deserted and I was circling it on my way home in the wee hours of the morning. I was horrified by the idea that the goddess—Cybele, for whom, in the night of time, the Korybantes danced and bled on the slopes of the Dindymon; Cybele, my queen, who stonily observed the sad path home from my own mysteries—was the center of celebration for a pilgrimage of danceless men. She was the custodian of the emasculated, the hermaphrodites, and the eunuchs, the mother of those who renounced grotesque masculinity and embraced the ferocity of women.

Porky was happy, but he seemed furious. I had always been scared by how those two emotions seemed to overlap when expressed by certain men. He was chanting the Real Madrid anthem while in the same breath bellowing, "Fuck Barça and fuck Cataluña." That stupid and sick hubris was terrifying to witness up close. In one of his fanatical convulsions, he decided it was appropriate to pick me up. He knelt down, wrapped his arms around my butt, almost placing his face in my crotch, and he stood up, taking me with him. He did it with ease; he was a brute. As he held me up, he mimed fucking me doggy style, exaggerating his thrusts and moaning exaggeratedly. I felt incredibly uncomfortable and violated, at the mercy of a guy who wasn't just playing some ridiculous game. He had an extremely acute predatory instinct, and this was his way of marking me and humiliating me. I saw it clearly. He lowered me when he was ready to, despite my twisting and kicking. Once I was back down on the ground, I glared at him with all the scorn I could summon into my pupils; he returned my gaze, laughing his ass off. I was about to cry; rage gripped the base of my neck like vomit that didn't quite come out. I held in the sobs as best I could. I didn't want to cry in front of him. We remained like that, still and mutually watchful until my father appeared, tapped me three times on the back, and said firmly, "Come on, let's get home."

I never was so grateful for him to make a judgment call. My father had always been a born protector, my mother too, except that she did it in a more spectacular fashion, like a large, noisy feline capable of biting the sky to insulate us from all evil. My father, although small in size, always had the poise of a large pachyderm; he was a wall between us and anything threatening. He had a very forceful energy that convinced everyone that it was not a good idea to test him.

I don't know what my father saw that day, but he acted immediately and without room for hesitation. He didn't intervene the way a father would with an adult son. I believe he perceived a very fragile displeasure in my expression; I don't know. No one came over to insist that we stay. There was no time; he grabbed me by the arm, and in what seemed to me like an instant, we were far from the crowd, returning home beneath the streetlights on Concha Espina.

"Don't hang out too much with that Piggy guy, okay?"

"Porky, Papá."

"Whatever, Porky, keep your distance from him."

And of course, I did. We bumped into each other at maybe one or two more games, and I avoided him best I could. He approached, knowing he repulsed me; he would glue his body against mine and breathe into my face and, after he'd had his fun, ignore me. Those few games were how long it took for me to stop going to the stadium, and more or less how long it took him to change grandstands, from the nosebleeds to the lower south seats. Gradually I abandoned the self-harm of watching games for camouflage. I did it subtly. Hardly anyone noticed, just my father; for him, I would have worked up some interest in watching some afternoon on TV at home, but luckily he started watching soccer at the bar with neighbors and acquaintances, and that small, empty nest of his didn't last long.

CALYPSO

Night, when it wasn't mine, wasn't night. Maybe just a sadistic version of the day, when disinhibition delineated the social hierarchies more cruelly. In that decade—the nineties—when behaviors relaxed as the day wore on, subtle aggressions turned fierce. I never understood why some people's best idea of fun was humiliating others. Yelling at women from cars was a typical warm-up for the groups of boys who went out partying, compelled by a strange demon of brutality. Even the good boys, especially them, put those intimidation rituals before their own well-being. Masculinity was a coercive force that caught up with everyone. It was impossible that such behavior was actually fun, beyond a surge of power that could be confused with joy, something similar to the effects of cocaine. They had to mark territory, laugh the loudest, create bubbles of adrenaline to ride out the night's early waves.

When I went out alone, I was very careful about my timings, when I left and when I came home; unlike what people always say, it was much safer closer to daybreak. The exhaustion attenuated any desire to pick fights, and almost everyone was wanting to get home and into bed, including the victimizers. Even still, not on a single one of those dawns, when I made a hideout in the gap between genders and feminized my appearance a few degrees, was I spared verbal attacks. I also endured more than a few physical intimidations, which I tried to stay ahead of by fleeing like an animal very familiar with its predator. Years of daily experience had taught me that sooner or later, my turn would come. Inhabiting the feminine, even intermittently— and my existence as a woman was as fleeting as ignis fatuus— activated the necessary corrective reprisals. My ghosts knew of this prophecy. Women, queers, and other existences that deviated from the masculine were marked as prey in the world of malevolent men.

My brother, Darío, was one of the good men. He was almost five years older than me and practiced a form of kindly and protective manhood, the heir to our father's pachydermic tendencies. Just by observing him, I was convinced that someday he would be a devoted father and an attentive and affectionate husband. Everything about him sketched those outlines of classic kindness and responsibility. He took care of me as much as he could, as much as I would let him, which wasn't much.

Men are taught to talk, not converse, and there was no way to bridge both the barrier of my fear and his reluctance to ask questions.

We were in a very famous club on Calle Valverde, a passageway that connected the Gran Vía to Malasaña that I knew very well. We'd gone out together, not something we did often, but that made us feel closer. He never made me feel uncomfortable, and I never saw him hassling anyone. We chatted, drank; I danced more than he did, and we let the night pass. That was a very popular place where you went to finish off the night; inside, you could find any combination of revelers. The Bardem brothers were there with a group of friends, and Shangay Lily surrounded by acolytes she towered over both in height and in sauciness. A random guy with his shirt unbuttoned and sunglasses on his head danced to techno, clapping and seeking out a complicity no one reciprocated. It was that kind of place where the night goes to die.

It was late, almost the hour when outside the sky's color must have been changing, when a blond woman approached us, with very messy curly hair, fair eyes that shifted to match the lights on the dance floor, and good height. I could guess what would happen next: she would say something into my brother's ear, holding a drink, he would respond, they would exchange a little more small talk, and they would end up kissing. Women really liked Darío.

"Hello, I'm Estrella."

I was slow to realize that she was talking to me, and I reacted clumsily, choking on a sip of my drink and coughing.

"Take it easy!" she said, laughing and patting me on the back as if she were a grandmother.

"Hello, Estrella, sorry—looks like I forgot to swallow."

"Is this your boyfriend?" she asked.

"No, no, he's my brother."

Darío laughed and gave us some space.

"Glad to hear it."

That was new. It wasn't strange for girls to take an interest in me, but quickly some glimmer of my true nature would end up arousing a very asexual tenderness in them. We weren't talking long before she kissed me; she tasted of alcohol and fruit. I kissed her back, as disconcerted as if it were my first kiss. In my head, there was a commotion like a silverware drawer being overturned—disaster, chaos, the unexpected, causing all sorts of turmoil. I maintained my composure on her lips, which were soft and very pleasant. I tried not to betray the alarm in my mind. My ghosts shrugged, not knowing what to say but not leaving, either; I reviewed lessons and desires and wondered if I wanted to do that or not. I did. But I didn't know how to. Estrella was clear on what she wanted, and she took me by the hand and led me to the exit, barely giving me time to say goodbye to my brother, who by that time was already on the other side of the club. He looked at me from there, grinning, and waved me off.

Estrella's studio apartment was in the Plaza de los Mostenses, which unfolded tightfistedly near the Gran Vía. It was a space that didn't really earn the name plaza and housed a very popular old market. It was Saturday morning, and there was the bustle of merchandise filling the stalls; it smelled of fish, tobacco, and sewers. The entrance to her building was right in front. We went up to the third floor and through a door you saw as soon as the elevator opened. Her apartment was a single square room, with windows onto the plaza, a sofa bed that was open and unmade, a small kitchen, a multipurpose table, and a bathroom. Before we lay down, I noticed a poster hanging on the wall that was the headboard: Coppola's *Dracula*.

"You're so cute," she said.

She kissed me slowly but deeply, opening her mouth wide and seeking mine out. Between kisses, she slid her face over my skin and whispered in my ear, aroused and sleepy. She placed herself on top of me and unbuttoned her blouse patterned with swallows. I wasn't able to anticipate it. I remained beneath her, my desire triggered but in some remote place, waiting for me to make an executive decision. I was consenting but not participating there on that mattress. Estrella was lovely; she had a rounded, warm body that wanted hands all over it. I decided to take a small step and caress her hips and belly; her breasts were too imposing for me to dare to touch them yet. My desire for sex was slowly but definitively awakening, with all the confusion that entailed. I knew how to act with men; with them, I had plenty of instinct and determination. I was never scared of making them uncomfortable, not because I didn't respect them, but because the boundaries were clear; I was sure our bodies were meant for each other. The prospect of desiring or falling in love with a woman was beguiling but always seemed too complicated. Only when I was underneath one who wanted me did I realize how nervous I was about making a mistake, a wrong step that would upset her, or surprise her, or scare her. I had spent my childhood dreaming of being pure and putting the women in my life on pedestals, making them the stars of a mythic, untouchable fantasy, and the situation I found myself in surpassed any I could have ever predicted. What was I? Who was I? Could I play the concubine with her and surrender like I did in the dark back rooms of bars, on narrow streets, in cars, in parks, or in my lovers' apartments? Would she desire me like that, or would she expect me to have the energy and demeanor of a flesh-hungry faun?

Our encounter was escalating, and Estrella took off her clothes and then mine. I wanted to connect with her and let myself go to the gynaeceum rooms where women rode one another till dawn, but I couldn't. I was pulling away helplessly like that childhood moon; the harder she pressed against me, the more she demanded of me, the more I distanced myself. The erection she'd provoked in me wasn't helping; it made me hyperaware of my body, of its smoothness and its protuberances. I couldn't go with the flow and join the beautifully slow undulations of Estrella's body. I felt I might be betraying the woman inside me, succumbing to the masculinity I denied with every fiber of my being. I was a celestial body blinded by the binary solar system around which I orbited, a male star and a female star, the same gravitational trap that kept me withdrawn inside my own skin, denying me the possibility of fucking another woman, whether I wanted to or not. Estrella was Calypso, and I was afraid to be Odysseus, afraid her hips would be the entrance to life eternal as a man.

When I gently pushed her off me and confessed that I could not go on, she embraced me with that tenderness I was used to getting from women and told me it was okay. I got dressed, apologized, and left with a knot in my throat. I heard her footsteps behind the door and her body dropping onto the bed.

I called my brother to come pick me up. He was there in a flash. As always.

EUGENIA

ugenia, nicknamed Caramel, began her workday near the Luna movie theater at dusk, where she made some cash for dinner and not much more giving sad hand jobs to old guys passing through the plaza before supper. In an hour or two, skulking in doorways, she took care of four or five customers who only needed an expert hand to remind them they still had feeling down there. Sometimes they would try to kiss her, and she'd pull her face away.

"Vicente, cut it out, for fuck's sake. Save that for your wife or someone who loves you."

She knew how to treat them; she knew how to treat everybody. She could be feisty when she wanted to, a vengeful saint capable of conjuring powerful ghosts who could summon the evil eye and sharpen her tongue. Which wasn't incompatible with having the biggest heart in the world. Her surly gaze, somewhat similar at times to María the Wig's, could detect tormented souls, sadness, and melancholy like a divining rod for loneliness. That's how we met.

I was heading up Calle Valverde towards the Plaza de San Ildefonso, and she was resting on the hood of a parked car on the corner of Puebla. She was wearing a white dress with a loose knit that revealed a lot of skin and kept her comfortable, the kind of thing you'd choose to wear when you knew you had hours of hard work ahead of you but you wanted to look divine and air out perspiration. She wore her thick black hair pulled back in an incredibly tight ponytail, revealing an enviable hairline. You couldn't help but notice her boots; I later learned that they had been her trademark since '84. They were tall and shiny, with high, thin heels. At first glance, you didn't notice she'd patched them up with black tape; when you got up close, you could see they were falling apart, but from a distance, they still looked good.

She was short, dark like Moroccan or Tunisian women often are, with a divine touch of Ivorian—hence her nickname, Caramel. Her eyes were large and round, well separated, which gave her face a smooth clarity. She was very thin and hadn't had anything done to her breasts; she was plenty satisfied with just letting the hormones do their thing. She had splurged on an ass that was perfect for mambo.

"This is from a doctor's office, maricón, not some basement," she would say, patting her backside. She had a nice, gravelly voice, which she described as "born to sing boleros."

She was already pretty old and ready to retire by the time we met; she said she'd saved up enough to quit working soon, although that day never seemed to come, and every evening around seven, she would renew her ritual of beauty and candles. She would light a few to whatever saint would ensure she had a profitable night and keep away anyone wishing to do her harm. It's not that she needed the intercession of any higher power to defend herself; she wore her chimera fierceness close to the surface, hard to define but impossible to miss. Eugenia—Caramel—was Medusa. She often mumbled to herself; that must be a sign of a sorceress. Perhaps what the uninitiated saw as a solo conversation was actually a witch negotiating small favors from invisible demons or saints.

I never knew where she was from originally. She left Latin America in the early eighties, which is like saying she came from Africa—a ridiculous, very European way of looking at continents several times the size of ours. Her accent was mixed; she covered it up very well and had done everything possible to sound like a Madrileña. That was a shame. Occasionally I thought I could detect some Caribbean silkiness in the music of her speech, but it faded quickly. She said that she'd had to leave her country because she was a tranny and a cannibal. The first time she told me that, I thought it was really funny, until I realized that she didn't seem amused; she remained serious and quickly curbed my laughter.

As she went through her nightly stations of the cross, from the Plaza de la Luna to Calle de la Ballesta, then to Calle del Desengaño, making a brief stop at Calle Valverde, where she found eager young customers, and then a final round on Hortaleza and Reina, where those who hadn't found anyone on Montera ended up. She would buy sandwiches to give to the youngest whores, girls from Eastern Europe whose pimps had them working all night with just a couple of bags of Doritos, Cheez Doodles, or some other twenty-five-cent snack in a bag. The pimps would often confront her, but she brushed them off easily.

"Am I in your territory? Did you pay for the sandwich? No, right? So fuck off, shitlicker, or I'll slice you from your cunt to your mouth."

That force of nature was about to walk into my life and set off an earthquake.

"You look terrible, maricón." Those were the first four words that Eugenia spoke to me that night on Calle Valverde. "Come here, come on over. I don't bite, at least not on Fridays."

Ever since a bad experience I'd had the year before, going out with some guys I never should've gone out with, had ended with me crying in the Casa de Campo park after learning that some bastards were calling the trans prostitutes shemales, I'd realized that I was much closer to those ladies than to anyone else I'd ever met. Some of the women who'd left an indelible mark on my life, even if I hadn't had much dealings with them, had worked in that profession. What I did on my sacred nights could be considered a form of tourism in their line of work; I offered up my body in exchange for attention and validation instead of for money. I also did it as a resuscitation ceremony. I don't know, I needed to feel like I was still alive and the best way I'd come up with was by placing myself in men's hands. This parallel between me and them, as silly as it may seem, worked for me for a while. It helped me to find a place until, instead of observing them and wondering about them, I started talking to them. That made them real people and not idols up on pedestals. I'd realized that glorification is another way of stripping someone's humanity.

I trusted Eugenia even before I knew her name. I approached just as she'd requested.

"All right, now what's going on with you, maricón." It was a question and a statement at the same time.

I could only answer with vagueness.

"Nothing, it's just late, and I'm tired . . ." A reference to myself in the feminine—"cansada"—slipped out, and I quickly corrected it to "cansado." "I was already on my way home," I lied.

"More than cansada—you look like you just buried your mother, gaylord. Come on, walk me to my door. I've got my pussy in my feet and my feet in my pussy. It's close by, on Calle Pelayo, by the Vulture."

"Oh, yeah. I know where that is."

"Of course you do, ya big poof," she said, bursting out laughing.

She grabbed my arm, and we walked slowly. Madrid in the hour right before dawn is a gorgeous city. Dirty and devious, without the spaciousness of Berlin or Barcelona, without their love of open space, but gorgeous in its own way. The street-lights' glow, contrasting with the constant gray of roads, side-walks, and walls, made things seem fleetingly gilded. It was the city where ugliness found a way to seduce. Narrow streets without any obvious charm held small treasures from bygone eras which somehow survived: button shops, drugstores that still stored their products in little wooden drawers, commemorative plaques for forgotten figures, gloomy little churches with religious sculptures that attracted unexpected devotion, porno theaters beside chocolate shops frequented by cheerful widows. Madrid was strange and had to be delved into thoroughly in order to unravel its secrets. Oblivious to its grand monumentalism, all of Madrid's reputation, all of its beauty, lay with its inhabitants, who, despite how they cast their votes, were incredibly welcoming. It lay in the professional waiters who were quick to serve but not servile; in the hundred and one instructions, confusing in their variety, that any Madrileño would give wayward tourists to ensure they reached their destinations; in the autumn in Retiro Park with kids picking dead leaves off the ground to show them to strangers; in the black roofs filled with mythology that no one even glanced at, because Madrid was built downward, designed to always keep your feet on the ground. The cacophony of shutters rising and people greeting one another first thing in the morning made me smile, and I was moved by the modesty of what the city offered, so far from other better-laid-out ones, and its childish need to captivate whoever passed through. I usually walked home because I loved Madrid; I recognized myself in how difficult it was to perceive its truth, in its elusive charm, and in how poignant its nooks and crannies could be. I couldn't escape being from Madrid just like I couldn't escape being trans. No matter how hard I tried.

"Don't you love the city at this time of day?" asked Eugenia.

"I was just thinking that; I find it very moving."

"*Moving*? That's a really pretty word. I like how you say that; tell me more."

No one listened like Eugenia; she was the best at feeding the conversational fire with the perfect interjections, adding little logs right when they were needed to keep it slowly burning.

"I don't know, well, I usually walk back home. I live really far from here, and I feel like the city is my accomplice when I cross through it; I have more time to be by myself. Being alone—sola, solo—gives me space to be moved, to get a little emotional. I don't know, it's silly, I guess."

"No, it's not, fairy. Something must be causing you a lot of pain for you to have that gaze and talk like that. I used to be that way. I won't tell you that it'll pass, because there's no magic that can take the place of wanting to do things or not wanting to. I will tell you that the world is real fucked up, really fucking fucked up, and filled with shitlickers wanting to beat the joy out of you; you already know that, but there are things you can do. Stop lugging around that baggage, and use what you carry inside of you. And if for now it's enough for you to walk around at night and cry like a puppy dog, then do it."

The street sweepers were slapping the streets with torrents from their hoses and making the ground shine as if it were paved with lightning bugs. There were hardly any cars passing as we crossed Hortaleza and reached Pelayo.

"Here it is. Wanna come up? I won't give you liquor, and I don't have much food. I can make you a nice hot chocolate that'll go down real smooth, and then you can go on your way, tranquila, tranquilo, however the hell you want." As she invited me up, she was already taking off her boots in the doorway. "Ay, maricón, my feet are killing me."

"Some other day. I want to get home as soon as I can. I don't think I'll walk today; this time with you was enough for me. Thank you so much, it's been really nice, and I'm so happy I met you."

"I'm usually around where you found me, and I almost

always end the night on Hortaleza. Come by and see me some-time. If you come early in the night, you'll find me in the Plaza de la Luna, and you can buy me a montadito. Ask the girls for Eugenia or for Caramel if you don't see me. Normally there's one who goes by La Cartier; she always knows where I am, ask her."

"And how will I know which one is La Cartier?"

"Oh, you'll know, trust me."

THE MOIRAI

Leaning against the wall of the San Martín de Tours church, where Calle Desengaño dies and Calle de la Luna is born, Raquel—La Cartier—was taking the last few drags on a cigarette and polishing off a can of orange soda. Of course I recognized her. She looked like one of those languid, excessive women in the poems of Baudelaire, an old widow who puts on all the jewelry she has and all the makeup she can lay her hands on to go out and get drunk in the cafés of Pigalle. Like that but from Segovia. She always wore a plastic tiara, which she defended as being of the very finest plastic, and a collection of costume necklaces of every color. Every finger had a ring on it, and her bracelets covered half of her forearms. Every time she moved her hands, which she did a lot, she produced a clinking that drove the other girls crazy. And when you could hear her but not see her, it meant she was working in some nearby doorway; when the rhythm accelerated, the girls would say that

La Cartier was about to show up because the jingle bells were almost done.

"Are you La Cartier, ma'am?"

"Ma'am? Don't be silly. Yes, it's me; what can I do you for, cupcake?"

She looked me over, incredulous; she knew how to spot a potential customer, and it seemed I didn't look like one.

"I'm sorry to bother you, ma'am— Oh, sorry! I'm looking for Eugenia; she told me to ask you if I didn't see her around."

"I've fuckin' had it up to here with La Caramel; she thinks I'm her lady chamberlain!"

I had trouble not laughing at the term "lady chamberlain," which I thought was actually a fabulous moniker that someone should snatch right up.

"Look, if she's not here, she must've stopped in the Portuguese bar, there on Hortaleza, next to the beefcake store; you know which one I mean?"

The beefcake store was a place that sold supplements for bodybuilders; pretty much everyone who knew Chueca was familiar with it.

"Yeah, I think I do. Thank you very much, Cartier; have a good night."

"Oh my, you're as courteous as the Civil Guard." She

winked at me. "Thanks, darling. You can also call me Raquel or Raquelilla."

I soon found the bar she was referring to, and there was Eugenia, drinking a coffee and flipping through a grease-stained newspaper. She was excited to see me come through the door, and I couldn't help but break out in a smile of pure peace. I'd thought about her often since our first encounter, and I'd prepared to see her again as if I were meeting up with a family member I was especially close to. One of those wise maternal figures, a godmother who teaches you important lessons you remember for the rest of your life. A woman I could learn from without having to do it in hiding.

"Hey, homy palone! So great to see you! Come in, have a coffee, and pay for mine; you heard me, maricón."

Visiting Eugenia became a mandatory pilgrimage that I found a way to do at least once a month. I would make sure our meetings coincided with the nights when I went out alone to indulge in my own mysteries. First a coffee and a chat with her, then whatever the night wanted to do with me. In my daytimes, everything was getting worse. The role of the good boy was becoming a cancer, and my dysphoria was leading me to fantasies of amputation, of rusty modifications of my flesh—nothing that had anything to do with surgical kindnesses or medical help. My body had developed according to what I demanded of it during the day, and the possibility of butchering it myself or putting an end to it all was never far from my mind. I was incapable of having calm conversations or controlling my emotions; I heard attacks in everything, or a chance for me to attack. I lied compulsively, and I couldn't keep track of what I'd said, not because I had a bad memory or was out of it, but just out of pure indifference. I couldn't care less about distancing myself from the people in my diurnal life or if they thought I was a hypocrite. I kept up some relationships as props, and I hated myself for it. My humanity, my goodness, the only thing I retained that was truly mine in both of those two lives, was dwindling, and I wasn't doing anything to stop it.

Eugenia reminded me that I was good; Eugenia tamed my attitude until it was as sweet as it should've always been, as came naturally to me, deep down. Eugenia was my pillar; she kept me in touch with what made me a woman and a human. I got in the habit of leaving early for my nights out, finding her and getting ready while we had some dinner or a drink. We frequented the same bars, where they already knew her and they ended up knowing me, too. They assumed I was just someone she'd taken under her wing, who was seeking a safe place to sissy it up once in a while, or I was learning the trade.

I would show up with my backpack and head into the bar bathroom first thing to change my clothes and shoes. Then I would sit down with her; we'd order some food, which I usually paid for with my earnings from the odd jobs I strung together while I decided what to do with my life—after all, I was taking up time she could be spending on the street— and I would put on my makeup at the table, between bites. We talked about everything. She would tell me anecdotes from her life, carefully chosen so as not to reveal too much; they were important things, but she never completely pulled the veil off her past. I came to understand that memory's folds are treacherous; they can release memories so vivid, they run the risk of trapping you in places you'd promised yourself you'd never set foot in again. Mostly she told me about her first years in Madrid, how long it took her to find her place, Spanish clients' obsession with hiding when they were with her, like frightened, irascible children incapable of confronting human truths such as pleasure. She said that was a reflection of the years of dictatorship, that everyone seemed childish and helpless—victims of a harsh, violent father—and in need of a lot of love to get over it, yet danger-ous because their immaturity had a lot of rage connected to it. When I tried to dig deeper into her past, she dodged me easily, and with love. As I rattled off my questions, her gaze shifted to one that broke my heart, to the sad little eyes of someone dancing a bachata alone in a ramshackle bar. We laughed a lot; she fixed my makeup, and I had to remind her that I was going out to dance and fuck, not to work with her, that I didn't need to paint myself up like a poisonous flower to attract drone bees.

"Your face will crack someday too, ya bitch," she'd say. "And then you'll remember me."

I told her everything. From the second time we saw each other, in the Portuguese bar, I knew that Eugenia was a unique and wonderful presence in my life that I had to take good care of. While Jay had led me by the hand to a moment of self-love, of euphoria, of a pearly life under the sun, Eugenia was a sorceress of listening, someone to whom I could pray the transvestite Ave Maria. Eugenia was the first woman who would hear my confession and respond with words of comfort, teaching, and support. Unbeknownst to her, I'd adopted her as my trans mother, cross-dressing role model, and friend. Sometimes Raquel, La Cartier, would join us, and another really fun woman named Paula, who they called La Chinchilla because of her fondness for faux fur. Paula'd had some bad experiences with *retouching*, which was how she referred to the injections of motor oil or old silicone that she'd gotten done in the late seventies in an apartment on Cava Baja. The ravages were very visible on her cheekbones, transformed into lumps. Her arrests during the time of the Law on Social Danger hadn't exactly helped maintain her sweet face intact, either. She was a kind, good woman, the least malicious of the three, although perhaps the wisest. She was too old and worn out to keep working, but she didn't have a pot to piss in, either; she depended on the help of the other two and took turns sleeping in their homes. She ate like a little bird and always took the leftovers from the bars, even if they were just tapas. Still, she went out every night to work with her head held high and looking for a good time. Inevitably, looking at her reminded me of Margarita, my Margarita. They shared the same tenderness, the same scars, and the same dignity. By that point, I was very ashamed of those ugly thoughts of repulsion that had coursed through my head as a little girl when I saw Margarita. In those bars on the border between Chueca and Malasaña, after learning that life was something much bigger than what I'd glimpsed in San Blas, those two women seemed like a paradigm of the beauty of survivors and, even in a hundred lifetimes, I would never be worthy of them.

Eugenia was Medusa on her own, and when they got together, the three of them were the Moirai, the Fates. I adored seeing them spin the threads of human destiny, so strong, so funny, so wise. They had that way of arguing that told a story of undeniable loyalty; the more outrageous insults they flung, the clearer it was that they would kill for each other. Eugenia always carried cough syrup in her bag because La Cartier had weak lungs from childhood malnutrition, many winters out on the street, and too much smoking. "Come on, ya old toad, have some of this; you're gonna hack up a lung if you keep coughing like that," she would say. And then she'd administer the cough syrup herself with the little plastic spoon included in the packaging.

At some point, Eugenia got so used to having me around that she even asked me to do up her ponytail. I felt like an altar girl for the Virgin of Macarena; it was a big deal to do Caramel's hair—her boots were her ruling scepter and her ponytail, her crown. Once she let me touch her hair, I knew that I had earned her trust forever. I would style her ponytail in the bars. I got pretty good at it; while I played with her hair, we would look at each other in the mirror and talk. Brushing out the queen of the trannies was an act of reverence and love. As I held the strands of her hair, I imagined a past in which my mother braided my hair or brushed it back into a ponytail. It seemed to me that when mothers comb their daughters' hair, they transmit an intangible love and a wordless beauty that couldn't be conveyed in any other way. Like how a sweater knit by your grandmother's knotted fingers carries the fragrance of time and loving care.

I opened up to her in a way I never had before. Even though I took up a lot of her time with my confessions, she never interrupted me, and she would wait until I finished before giving me notes, offering up advice, disagreeing, telling me I was wrong, or simply nodding. She was never condescending with me, and she reminded me of the importance of responsibility, of not leaving everything to fate, because fate was never a friend to women. She perfectly understood my fears, my defense mechanisms, and my pain; she would listen and honor them, but she didn't stop there. She always added a next step, an "And what do we do with that?," a way out, no matter how tortuous. With little ceremony, she would leave me bits of hope on those bar tables. That was something I'd never known.

Even though I never came right out and said that I was explaining my trans life to her, that was clear from the very beginning. Eugenia took care of me by allowing me time to find euphemisms. She addressed me in the feminine but allowing the possibility that it was just pure camp, so I wouldn't feel exposed. I wanted to keep talking to her and offer myself up whole on her altar for a full blessing. Months passed, almost a whole year, until she sensed—with no questioning beyond her witchy gaze—that my defenses were low enough for her to bring it up without beating around the bush. We were in our usual bar, her with her recently coiffed, high ponytail and me applying makeup with a portable mirror I could place on the table. We were waiting for them to bring us an order of patatas bravas, which she loved, and a couple of beers with lemon.

"Homy palone, you can't go on like this."

"Like what, Eugenia?"

"Like this, girl, and you know it." I looked away from the little mirror and at her. She continued, "It's fine with me if you want to fuck the whole neighborhood painted up in drag;

you go for it—when I was your age, not a day went by when I didn't get my booty clap on—it's not that, marica, it's not that. If you'd thrown yourself under a bus the day we met, well, I would've chalked it up to another fag who couldn't take it anymore, a lost soul lost forever, that's just some people's path. . . . I would've lit a candle for you and forgotten you." She paused when the waiter came with our drinks and food. "You'll have to forgive me, marica, but it hurts me to see you come in here dressed like one of the johns on Calle Valverde, then go into the bathroom and come out the way you come out, shaking your hips and with a different voice. And you're only in there for ten minutes, girl. Ten minutes! And that doesn't scare me as much as the road back, the one I don't see, when you take off the makeup and the heels and you get dressed again for the other side. That's death, marica, that's death."

We had talked a lot over that year, and I had seen her in most every mood, but never so moved. She remained firm. Her voice didn't tremble; she spoke each word with the proper combination of scolding, concern, and affection, but she was having more trouble than usual holding back the tears that flooded her eyes without spilling.

"I know what you've told me; I've listened to it all. I understand, marica—how could I not understand? But you can't go on like this; you think I don't see the toll it's taking on you? From one month to the next, I see how your weight goes up and down, how your little eyes droop, and I know that's not all, girl. It looks like all the saints and demons have abandoned you; they're not listening to my prayers. My matches go out, and I don't light more than three; it's better not to have them by our side than to force them to be there."

I didn't know anything about saints or demons, but by that point, I knew Eugenia well enough to understand that I shouldn't discount her relationship with them. I'd learned that if she felt it was essential to add them to her list of concerns about me, they would stay there alongside the other fears.

"Eugenia, I just can't. I'll never be able to. I'm so scared."

"It's really scary, girl, how could it not be, have you seen them out there? But what choice do we have, what else can we do?"

I could never have had a conversation like that with anyone. Eugenia's questions, her statements, were so spot-on that they left me completely naked, and there was nothing in this world I feared more than nakedness. Facing up to the truths of both my flesh and my soul. As she spoke to me, she was giving me a landing pad, a warm, dimly lit space without the lacerations of the sun or the dreamy states of the moon. A place where, finally, naked and exposed, I could rest. I cried, I wept, I smudged the only eye I had put makeup on, and I couldn't stop throughout the entire conversation.

"I do my nights," I began, stammering, trying to control my

hiccups. "I find a man, two, or three. Whatever I need to end up feeling empty. I don't use them; I give them back everything they give me, in spades. While I'm with them, I imagine that they love me, that they would die for me, that I'm a goddess, a queen, a priestess, a concubine. I would die for them while they devour or dominate me. You know, Eugenia? I find so much light in that submission. That's horrible to admit, and I know that it's a bad way to start out as a woman, putting my desire, however fleeting, into the hands of men. But I can't do it alone. I can't even touch myself alone in my room. As soon as I run my hand over my chest or pelvis, I shrink like a worm, Eugenia. I lose my ability to fantasize; I'm left blank and trembling, as if my body disappeared, as if it were headed to some cosmic dumpsite for bodies that don't belong anywhere. But when one of those blessed men puts his hand on the back of my neck and sticks his cock in my mouth, or when I have them inside me, new outlines appear before me; they sketch out a body that I like or can imagine liking. I've never known anything else. I never learned to define myself with loving words; I need desiring hands on me for that. God, this is embarrassing to say out loud, Eugenia. I'm dying of shame."

"Sweetheart, nothing shameful about it. Some tall, dark, and potbellied guy can reach that place your pride can't, and he reminds you why hanging on in this world is worth the effort. You don't need to make excuses for yourself around me; where

I come from, they're still waiting for first-wave feminism. The thing is, what comes next, what happens after that? Why do you keep kidnapping yourself?"

"Because I'm really scared."

"We already know that, marica, but what you're doing to yourself is torture, and it doesn't work. How long are you going to keep this up? Do you have any other plan? Because this one isn't working. Look at you, for fuck's sake, you can't even talk about it without crying. You can't just play at being a woman. We are women; we can't help it. You're proof of that. Putting on makeup and shaking your ass in heels a couple of weekends a month isn't being a woman; it's an escape, a Band-Aid, glibness that, sure, liberates you for a little while. It has its place, but it's costing you your life; I've been there and I respect it, but it's a sham. The woman inside you, the real one, is still trapped between narrow walls, and she's going to suffocate. And when she suffocates, that's it, marica, you're gone. No one can save you then. The other one, the soulless one in a button-up shirt and with a deep voice, is a dead man walking."

Eugenia—Caramel—really had some magic on her side that made her see things that nobody else could see. She had entered into that narrow world of mine with precise metaphors and had been able to see the corpse that walked during the day. Eugenia had reduced me to dust in order to give me a new life. She was playing with my silver thread and twisting it to her will; she could read in its strands and coarseness the smallest details, the things no one knew about me. She was uncovering everything. She paused to eat and drink a little, then wiped her mouth with a paper napkin and kept talking.

"You've tried to stay macho every possible way; from what you've told me and what I can see, you've tried harder than most. Congratulations on that; it takes real determination to get to where you have. I see you breaking down, from one month to the next, how your gaze grows absent. I already told you, poof, it scares me, and I'm not scared of anything. I'm not telling you you have to do something right now; I'm not telling you you have to do anything, but I am asking you to keep it in mind and stop playing with dolls in the little time you let yourself have out in your prison yard."

"And what do I do, Eugenia, where do I start?"

"Start by asking that question, for example. You don't have to go running to the doctor tomorrow; give yourself time to think about whether that's your path. That is a relief but not a cure. I'm not saying you have to gather up your family when you get home and tell them everything; you have your reasons for not doing that. Sometimes they surprise you, but you know who you live with, for better and for worse. That's nobody else's business; there are plenty of corpses that turn up under bridges over some idea of the truth. Come to terms with it yourself, not the way you have up until now, only daring to face who you are when you're hiding in the corners, like the cowardly men who want us but would rather kill us than walk through the park on our arms. Don't be your own pimp, marica. Don't let some jerk dominate you like that. Don't do that to yourself. That is the submission that kills us. Inside and out, the submission of cowardly men. Not what happens with the tall, dark, and potbellied who shake your tits with their belly thrusts. If you need to keep being the Pomba Gira of the back rooms, I'll be here to have dinner with you every night and lay flowers at your feet, but I would love for you not to need me, that you did it because that was what you felt like doing, that you were going after what you wanted. Everything tastes better that way, believe me."

"Have you ever had one of those, Eugenia? A pimp or a man like that, inside you or out."

"Yes, marica. My father."

"Oh, God, I'm so sorry, Eugenia. And what happened?"

"I ate him. Go on, finish your dinner; it'll do you good."

LA CHINCHILLA'S WINGS

The only time I ever tasted Eugenia's cooking was the night we held a wake for Paula, La Chinchilla. They'd taken her to the South Morgue in Carabanchel. Raquel had taken care of the paperwork so Paula would have access to public funeral services. During the evening, some of the other girls had come by, two or three clients she'd had for more than two decades, and Pepo, the waiter who'd been serving her warm milk with a drop of espresso every night before she went to sleep, ever since she arrived in Madrid. The men didn't stay long; they came through to pay their respects and left soon after, as if shame was rushing them. Eugenia had put out some plates on the table with a red rice that was delicious; banana-and-margarine sandwiches cut in fours, English style; and some grapes. Eugenia had found Paula sitting in the rain on the steps to a doorway on Corredera Baja, still, almost completely upright, her only concession to death just pure stillness. Eugenia hadn't finished calling her by her name when she realized that Paula was already in tranny heaven; that blessed soul couldn't have gone anywhere else. Eugenia phoned for an ambulance and then sat down by her side. She had leaned Paula over, placing her small dead head onto her lap, and like that, Eugenia stroking the little hair Paula had left, getting soaked under the downpour, they waited together for the doctors, police, and whoever else had to come.

Besides the food, Eugenia had put together an altar with a photo of Paula in a frame she'd glued some white carnations to. Right in front of it, on the table, she had placed a couple of wooden coins, a small bottle with essential oils warmed by a little tea light, a beeswax candle, a pigeon feather, and the bone of a sparrow's wing.

"I'd like to put a bracelet on her altar, is that okay?" La Cartier asked Eugenia when it was just the three of us.

"I wish you wouldn't, Raquel; these things are supposed to be done a certain way."

"Whatever, bitch, what harm would a bracelet do? I'll put a little one."

"Come on, give me one, that red one on your left arm."

"Oh, but that's a good one; it's real crystal."

"Maricón, don't get cheap now; shit, she's not even cold yet! Give me the bracelet!"

It was hung on one corner of the frame; the red beads reflected small glimmers onto Paula's face. Their size and gleam varied as the candle's flame moved. It was pretty.

They cremated her first thing in the morning. It was also raining and very windy. Eugenia said that was good because her spirit would travel upwards faster and leave the earth. I imagined Paula, La Chinchilla, flying over us all, with a white fur coat and huge wings.

After the cremation, we took the metro back to Chueca. The plaza that gives the neighborhood its name was still tidy, the only life a few passersby hidden beneath their umbrellas, on their way nowhere. We went into the bar on the corner of Augusto Figueroa for breakfast; I had never been in there, and they didn't go often. It was an ordinary bar; there were a few customers slowly sipping their coffees and, once in a while, dipping in a churro or a piece of toast. They had the unhurried calm of regulars; just by looking at them, I could tell that they'd been there the day before at the same time, occupying the same spots and eating the same breakfast. A radio was playing; although not very loud, it imposed itself on the customers. They barely spoke, and those who did spoke softly. I ordered coffees and toast with butter and jam for all of us. Eugenia and Raquel hadn't spoken a single word on the way home. They were tired and extremely sad. I was sad for them; of course I'd grown fond of Paula and was feeling the pain of her death, but in that moment, I was more concerned for the living. The Moirai had lost their source of tenderness, the one who threaded the needle carefully and mediated between the two Furies. Besides, Eugenia and Raquel had lost their elder, their patient rock, the one who listened to the thunderbolts and responded with kindness. They, along with some others, constituted a family that was shedding its petals, because time is a bastard and comes for everyone. But the three of them had held on as they watched others leave, gripping one another's arms tightly, holding one another up, believing that their way of loving one another would save them from having to experience loss again. Paula was sick, tired, and old; her death was logical but not fair. Nobody knows how strong the love of a trans family is.

"You know what's the worst part of it for me?" Eugenia broke the silence that was crushing us. "That she was never happy. Never. Paula had the toughest life of anyone I've ever met, and damn if we don't take some shit, but I've never seen anything like what she went through. And she didn't deserve a life like that. She didn't deserve it. She was born dirt-poor; they beat her senseless since she was a little girl. She came to Madrid, and it wasn't a month before they charged her under the Law on Social Danger, sending her to jail. Again and again. Outside, she was a whore, and inside, a slave. She was raped by the guards, the thieves, the murderers, the terrorists, the pimps, the political prisoners, and the horses they rode in on. All those beatings destroyed the rest of her face, what she hadn't messed up herself with those shit retouchings. My Paulita, so many years sleeping on the street and so many days without a single meal. She never made enough to live on, and damn if she didn't have guts. Did you ever see her cry even once? Be in a bad mood? Sad? Well, neither did I, marica, neither did I. Isn't that right, Raquel?"

"Not once. Almost fifteen years we knew each other and every day, singing softly to herself and with 'Ay, sister, don't let it get you down' on her lips."

"She seemed very happy with you two," I said to them.

What else could I add that wasn't just empty words? Their world was a world I had barely glimpsed.

Even though I loved Eugenia with my whole heart, I was a guest, not a member of the family, not a legitimate heir to their legacy. I didn't know the bitter side of their precious lives beyond a few anecdotes they'd told me. I was their daughter, but they weren't my mothers. Eugenia had saved my life and sorted it out for me somewhat; at least, she'd given me a real reason to stop hurting myself so much. I had learned a lot from her, from them; they were the first coven of women I belonged to, without distance, without hiding. I would've liked to have had a similar impact on their lives, to have shared in equal exchange, but with them, I learned that we daughters are always indebted, that we cannot give back what we're given, because that wouldn't be natural. Our mission is to pass on what we've been imparted to other women, whoever they may be. I learned that genealogy, as an inherited love, is a waterfall that only flows downwards.

WE MEET AGAIN

t was Christmas, and I had a lot of things to do. The last few years, I'd looked for jobs I could juggle with my studies despite the failures. I was getting through classes as best I could given my mental state, and I finished high school and finally passed my university entrance exam at an age when it should've been long behind me. I was considering preparing to take a public service exam; my parents thought that if I didn't have some support to anchor me, my life was going to be a disaster. Maybe they didn't know what was going on, but they knew my life wasn't going well. The idea of being a civil servant was completely repugnant to me; I didn't see myself capable of preparing to obtain a position like that, or making any commitments to a future that was still murky. I took whatever jobs I could, got some money together, spent it, and went looking for the next thing. Instead of aspiring to a life in public service, I registered to study history. It matched my need—that or philology was the logical continuation of my childhood love for myths and legends. Throughout my life, I'd only known the perspective of the past, and history seemed like a way to be consistent with that. If I could, I would specialize in medieval history. Otherwise, I would tear out every page of my life one by one until none were left.

I had saved more money than usual working at a moving company. It was hard work. They paid well, but there wasn't much time to socialize—it was nonstop, and we went from house to house. We loaded, unloaded, and started all over again. At the end of the day, they handed us an envelope, and we showed up the next day or not. There was no contract and no commitment.

I was not doing well—far from it—but that conversation with Eugenia had opened up doubts and paths. I decided to stop hurting myself so much and decrease the demands of my closet. I tried to make peace with my body by using it, appreciating its functionality and its ability to do hard things, but I was still far from forgiveness. That curtain between my flesh and me had to remain drawn; if I paid attention to what was behind it, catastrophe was sure to follow. I had only one way to commune with my skin, and it was the same as ever: away from the sun and its directives.

My day-to-day relationships continued to be disastrous, but I had cleared some space in my circle of acquaintances until I'd found an almost placid solitude. Having fewer people around me meant less staging. I just had a couple of girlfriends; finally I had girlfriends who, if I put in a lot of effort, I could imagine trusting at some point in the future. At least around them, I didn't have to set into motion the entire farce of the walking dead.

At the end of that year, I wanted to give good gifts. I'd already bought and hidden the ones for my family, but I was especially excited to buy some new boots for Eugenia. So she could retire the ones she always wore, make a mausoleum for them if they were in one piece, and give the queen a new scepter. I found a very similar pair at Chocolate, a shoe store for drag queens, strippers, whores, trannies, trans women, faggots, and anyone with enough bravura to wear the kind of heels they sold. I chose that store for its style, not its large sizes; Eugenia was petite and had small feet. I went to buy them dressed befittingly, no lies; they were important objects, and I didn't want to stain them with hypocrisy. They were for Eugenia.

Scared and extremely cautious, I nonetheless sought to take Eugenia's advice beyond the realm of inner healing. It wasn't something that could be done with mere words; it required reparative actions. I had built up a huge debt with myself that continued to grow and that I would be wise to pay down, so I began to conquer the daytime. I gradually socked away clothes like an ant: a skirt on sale one day, a clearance gown another, shoes from goth stores—which were the least complicated fashion spaces in terms of gender in the late nineties—and other items like that. I followed my same nocturnal routines: I would leave home with my backpack loaded up and head into the city center to the bars that were used to my costume changes, put on my makeup while I drank a couple of coffees, and go walking into the dusk.

The first time I went out on the street in a dress and makeup without any ambiguities, the first time I presented fully as a woman in public without the aesthetic escape valves that could be used to justify my appearance as merely effeminate, was a moment of power when there was no inertia or fear that could stop me. I had never felt like that before. The euphoria that I'd felt the night I confessed to Jay came back, multiplied a hundredfold. It was an adult euphoria, a happiness that overcame any look I might get; for once in my life, I felt that I was above hatred, shame, and prejudice. I wanted to be right there more than anywhere else; I wanted to be myself without fantasizing about fairy transformations. Every time my heels hit the ground, it was a victorious song, and I felt that the stars were aligning to offer me a glimpse of divinity. I was alive and driving my own heart to keep beating, instead of me dragging it along and waiting indifferently for it to stop. What for other women was an imposition was for me a conquest. Women weren't bees that all drank the same nectar; liberating ourselves, opening ourselves to the world, reclaiming the space we were owed, could be done from very different positions, and they were all good. That was mine, feminine and proud.

The first time I saw myself reflected in display windows and bus shelters, even though I was still afraid, was all adrenaline and resolve. The ritual involved in getting dressed up, applying my face, and presenting myself to the world was a sort of transubstantiation. A ghostly life's passage to corporeality.

It took a lot of bravery to compose myself in front of the mirror as someone who understood herself and to transfer that intimacy into the public sphere; it required all the strength I had. Because of that colossal demand I was making on myself, it would take very little for me to get badly hurt. I never felt so strong and so vulnerable at the same time. How could something so beautiful, something so personal and so extraordinary to share with the world, something that vibrated with pure joy, be perceived with such hostility out there?

It happened several times, not too many; those nights out meant setting into motion a variety of safety protocols that required very concrete conditions that didn't often come together. But they sometimes did, and a part of me hoped to unload the cadaver covering me sooner rather than later. The darkness was still there and the self-loathing too, but I had tasted the fresh air, an air that I had procured for myself by kicking like crazy from the depths, and I didn't want to give that up, even if it was in small doses and occasionally.

As a result, my nights improved. I heeded Eugenia and began to contemplate them from a place of desire, more a whim than a necessity. The urgency waned slightly, and what was left was the banquet and the divine pact between me and the men.

The boots were perfect. Above the knee, with a heel that was a Gorgon fang, shiny as oil and surely more comfortable than the wrecked ones my Caramel walked on every night. They wrapped the enormous box for me with the most ordinary wrapping paper I'd ever seen, and they placed a fuchsia lace bow on one corner. It was perfect. I wanted to kiss the salesclerk.

I left Calle Hortaleza, where the shoe shop was, and headed to the Gran Vía, swinging the bag. I felt like taking a long walk; night had fallen earlier, and it was cold, my ideal walking conditions. I was wearing wide-heeled boots, a tight black dress with a mermaid cut, and a three-quarter-length coat. I had let my hair grow out and I could already make a small bun, and I liked how the loose locks that weren't long enough to pull back framed my face. I had done a very deep black smoky eye and wore dark lips the burgundy hue of rotting red roses.

The city was teeming with people who'd come out to shop

and stroll. Winter looked good on Madrileños; they took over the city center just for the fun of it, when really most shopping could be done in any of Madrid's neighborhoods. Coming to the center was a tradition that didn't require extra spending: a moment of strolling, visiting the stalls in the Plaza Mayor, crossing through the Puerta del Sol, making fun of the unrepentant creepiness of Cortylandia's automaton Christmas spectacle, going along Montera and Gran Vía to Callao, and getting a little bit chilly before warming up in one of the cafés with the excuse of needing the restroom. The display windows gleamed and illuminated the city with that cheesy, exaggerated aura that suited it so well. Its skin had always been gray and lacked the variety of textures of other, much more beautiful places. In Madrid, you had to focus on all the things that were added to the space: the trees, the lights, its traditional denizens, things that didn't beautify a city but made it comfortable. Madrid was that beat-up sofa that really should be replaced but is so comfy and has so many memories attached to it that no one could bear to kick it to the curb, and instead they just keep replacing the cover. Through my smoky eyes, in my high heels and black dress, I was momentarily freed of the burden of carrying around a corpse, free of the weight of a moon that, on the way home those nights in the garden of earthly delights, had illuminated everything as if it were a theater of death or a macabre masquerade. I walked through in order to be alone; those streets I had traveled along so many times looked different, new, real. I passed people of flesh and blood; I could look into their eyes and see life in them.

My existence up until then had consisted of placing a mask over everyone, in harmony with my excruciating need to be hidden. A monstrous *commedia dell'arte* where all touching was off-limits, where everything was costumes and white gloves. In that moment, stripped naked of lies, dressed as myself, some people scared me, and I could sense their disdain, but I did so without the need to interpret it, without hearing it inside, without shrinking into recesses of my consciousness. I looked life in the eye with my head held high, proudly exposed, showing myself completely and living the most authentic and intimate experience possible there, in the center of Madrid, in full view of thousands of people illuminated by Christmas neon. I no longer walked alone.

I couldn't get enough of the streets, and when I reached the Plaza de España, I decided to keep going; the weight of my backpack and Eugenia's boots weren't enough to hold me back. I needed to keep filling my lungs with air.

The Plaza de España formed a real border between Gran Vía and Calle Princesa that became clear as soon as you crossed the plaza with its cube sculpture. The city's rhythm slowed, the sounds muffled, and there were fewer people strolling. It was a class border. Gran Vía wasn't a place you lived in—perhaps in the adjoining streets and neighborhoods, which prior to gentrification were among the poorest in Madrid. Gran Vía was a place you went to; people came from all over the metropolitan area, returning to their district or town at the appropriate time and probably not setting foot in the center for a while after that.

The west was another story: a conservative, wealthy area with little interest in mingling with the rest of the city except to colonize it if there was something there they wanted. They had plenty of their own infrastructure and commercial offerings; they didn't need to deal with long lines of people from what they considered to be worse neighborhoods. The stretch of Princesa that fed into Moncloa was pleasant for strolling— all the upper-class areas were. The streets were wider, and since their denizens could allow themselves to behave however they felt like upon leaving their neighborhood, they usually displayed perfect civility within it. Until they detected you didn't belong there.

One thing I had quickly learned when walking as a woman was to wear my headphones so no one would approach me, but without music playing so I could remain alert. The logical personal space didn't apply to women, who could be interrupted or bullied freely, with none of the problems that came with behaving like that towards a man.

I was so happy that night! I felt really pretty, and I'd found the perfect gift for someone I adored, so I decided to ignore my usual precautions and play a couple of songs on the last stretch of my walk. The idea was to get to Calle Fernández de los Ríos, which I knew well because my mother worked in a house there, cleaning, cooking, and minding the children of a military family, and walk to the end where I'd get in the metro at the Iglesia stop and go back to San Blas.

"This Charming Man" was playing when I got to that street; I was smiling and a bit giddy with euphoria. I could feel my dress rubbing against my back and my chest; it was similar to the high you get when it's really cold and you crawl into bed and have to warm up the sheets with your body, that anticipation of a comfort about to envelop you, that makes you start giggling uncontrollably. I struggled to hold back a loud laugh of pure happiness.

The first impact was confusing. I didn't have time to think or get my bearings. My body pitched from left to right as if pulled by an invisible horse. I rolled down some stairs in slow motion; time seemed to stretch and shrink meaninglessly to the whims of my adrenaline, and I seemed to be submerged in a strange dream. I stopped rolling and felt a stabbing pain in my ribs, and another, and another. I could barely lift my head, but I could clearly see someone with his face half-covered kicking my side with military boots. The blows started to rain down from everywhere, and soon it stopped hurting. My headphones had fallen off, but I kept them firmly attached to my coat, and I could hear the music somewhere far away, as if behind a thick curtain. I covered my face and tried to curl up into a ball, but the blows were doing their job, and my body no longer belonged to me.

I tried to get up two or three times, but my legs buckled as if they had no joints. Running away was never a possibility. I thought about Eugenia's boots, hoping they had been left behind on the stairs and were still intact. She really needed them. My mouth filled with blood I couldn't swallow, and it made me retch. I vomited it all up, on my knees, trying to hold up my torso by planting my elbows on the ground.

"The faggot's gonna puke up his liver! Kick him there!"

Everything was happening very slowly; I had time not only to think but to think rambling thoughts. The voice encouraging them to kick my liver out was a familiar one, but it soon blended in with other voices, of a group of men, more than seven but less than ten. From the ground, they were almost all backlit, and I couldn't count them.

My dress was pulled up and I was cold—that meant they were no longer beating me. One of them brought the end of a baseball bat to my ass and told the others he was gonna stick the whole thing up me.

"Fuck no, that's disgusting, then you take it home all covered in faggot shit," replied another.

They hovered above me for a while. I tried to sit up or get

on my knees again, but one of them would put his boot in my face and push me down every time I tried.

"Where you going, bitch? We're still deciding if we should kill you."

Inside myself I heard doors slamming, blows like wood banging together. My hope faded as if the spotlights in a theater were going out one by one. A sun demon was waiting to laugh at me on the other side of the blood.

I saw Eugenia's face before a mirror, illuminated by a candle. I saw her grow pale and spit blood. She saw me, fully dressed as a man, turning my back on myself and disappearing down the street as I whistled a childish song. I saw the moon, I saw its face, I saw its scythe, and it was crying for me; I saw a circle of the dead trying to speak to me from their tongueless mouths; I saw my dragon-men dancing as if for the last time, I saw them kiss one another, I saw them take off one another's clothes, I saw them surrender themselves to one another on a bed of flowers; I saw my entire life drifting away from me; I saw all the women of the world waving goodbye to me; I saw my brother, the penultimate good man under the sun, searching for me in the mist; I saw my mother crying over me, covering me with her body, her hair a mess, her eyes swollen, slobbering and unable to call out my name because I didn't have one.

The last thing I saw before vanishing into the darkness was a pair of small, almond-shaped, intensely blue eyes looking into mine.

"*Sieg Heil*, bitch." A hot lick on my cheek, a blow to my jaw. Then, darkness.

"You're so bad, Pork."

And nothing more.

How can you describe nothingness, how can you remember a dead end, how? They took everything from me, and there wasn't a single ember left to stoke up. The coven was over, the high-heeled pride was over, the closet shut over me like a coffin. Goodbye to all that. Goodbye to my life. From a depth deeper than ever, I heard the spheres moving, but I couldn't see them; I heard the dance of the tides, but I couldn't join in. There below, where the light didn't reach, where all that remained were illusory shimmers, I settled for making them my sky and stars. All the voices reached my abyss muffled; the questions had no face nor purpose, and I answered yes to them all. In that savage darkness moved forces I did not comprehend; dead bodies, thrown from the surface, sank, and I fed on them with the hunger of a horrendous deep-sea fish. My flesh grew cold; my heart was inertia and vagueness. I was stalled in an interminable sobbing that produced no effect on the waves of emptiness; my lover was silence, and I disgusted myself. The moon didn't reach me there, either, nor the tyrannies of the sun; you cannot count nothingness. It's beyond you.

No one could look me in the eyes during that time. No one cared enough to descend to the depths where names are forgotten. If I could've exchanged one glance, just one, I would've had a reason to reach my hand out into the void, waiting for someone to take it in theirs. But that never happened. What did come were the nightmares: flickering lights, white layers, and broken glass on my skin. More questions to answer yes to. The face of my brother desperately searching for me on the surface of an ocean he didn't understand. Other faces to answer yes to every question. Yes, yes, yes. The sense that someone was taking my place and rifling through my drawers, my room, my flesh, my affections.

The nature of the depths is what it is; you can't ask the abyss to be anything more than a darkness that swallows up everything, one in which nightmares are glimmers that also become diluted over time, one that blots kindness.

If it's possible to travel along the surface of nothingness, I began to do that, the way that mold moves or some spurious coral feeds on darkness. A step towards nowhere, two steps, three steps, dragging my feet and leaving furrows in the cold sand, sidestepping bodies consumed by my sick silver teeth, my steps devoid of memory and awareness. I ascended blindly along unfamiliar walls with protrusions that scratched my flesh, until I reached an area where the waters were less murky, where I could finally sense light above me.

I kicked. I kicked instinctively, furiously, hungrily, for vengeance, for love, because I couldn't die like that in the world's memory before dying in my own consciousness. I ascended higher, higher, bluer, more lights playing. I felt the water growing cooler and caressing my skin, welcoming me. I could almost reach the surface as if it were a promised heaven, I saw spectral faces awaiting me, I saw the backlit silhouette of a dead body bobbing, I reached it, I went through it, I got inside, and I took a gulp of air that almost shattered my lungs. I opened my eyes.

And thirteen years passed.

COLD SKIN

hardly ever set foot there; at most I would visit my parents once a month, but I was witness to the enormous changes that were happening in San Blas. It had grown old, and there was no trace of life left on its streets. It had become residential according to the tastes of conservative governments, promoting a fictional middle-class lifestyle in the form of urban expansions with shared swimming pools on the outskirts. That sort of construction hadn't reached the heart of the neighborhood, but the ways of life and aspirations that came with it had. Most of the old blocks of apartments had been demolished years ago, and the inhabitants, my parents included, relocated into taller buildings of orange brick, with wide entrances and landings. The apartments were much more spacious than the ones they'd left behind, two or three bedrooms, with drywall divisions and kitchens big enough for a small table.

San Blas was no longer the same brutal, tender place it once was. The heroin had done its job and then receded like a toxic tide. Most of the neighbor ladies I remembered were dead or so old they couldn't even recognize their own streets anymore. The networks of small kindnesses had been unraveling slowly with each funeral; the new families were hardly ever even seen on the landings, entryways, or the few shops that remained. My generation and some of the previous ones, who were expected to take up the mantle and preserve some of the neighborhood spirit, had fallen by the wayside. All that was left of them was the memory held by their parents, who were drained from weeping. The paradigm had shifted, and life happened behind closed doors. This wasn't good or bad necessarily—just kind of sad from the perspective of a life lived in community. But every look back into the past tends to sweeten situations that are still tinged with bitterness. It was true that there was less class consciousness and that you couldn't expect to ever again see the neighborhood united and defending itself against the bosses' maneuvers or the abuses of the right-wing politicians who had already devoured the entire city. If you wanted to scare up some nostalgia, that was the surefire way: dredging up workers' solidarity. But that was where it ended.

The cruelty had diminished, and while it was no paradise of harmony and coexistence, that small space of leniency allowed other queer lives to bloom, lives that hadn't had that option before. They weren't many, and they weren't obvious, but they were there, living behind closed doors but with the choice to occupy a small part of the public space if the need arose. It had been a very bitter pill to realize that, at least there, you couldn't have both things, and that being different was something that required a certain isolation to show its face, that alliances had to be sought out elsewhere. While as a five-year-old, I wondered why women didn't seem to be part of the "comrades," as a trans woman, as a poof in practice, I had accepted it almost naturally. I had developed my working-class consciousness knowing that the men and women of my class, my comrades, would let me fall time and time again before modifying a part of the common struggle to offer me a safety net.

I had finished college and stopped flitting from one job to the next. I had also moved out, although maybe it was a stretch to say I was independent when I was sharing an apartment with three or four others. I had been working as a bookseller for ten years, a poorly paid occupation with crushing hours that barely allowed me to live in a Madrid relentlessly hostile to the working poor. Selling books didn't make me the happiest person in the world, but it kept me close to the written word, to the lives of others, be they real or legendary, which I needed since I lacked a life of my own. I wasn't particularly good at my job, but I wasn't the worst, either; I dealt with the logistical aspects as best I could, and I think I was able to transmit some of my love for the stories that moved me. I had no other magnetism working for me. I was never like the booksellers I learned the ropes from, who could guess what readers needed as soon as they walked through the door and seemed to be speaking a different language that contained all the stories. I loved books as much as they did, and I tried to learn that language of seduction, but the intelligence and perspicacity needed to master it were not in my wheelhouse, so I would listen and experience the profession through them. I did what I knew how to do: lean into a world that wasn't mine, allowing myself to be permeated by what I could touch and observing from a prudential distance what I couldn't. My life was not a life, but in the bookstore, I had all the stories within reach, unending fantasies with which to nourish my infinite capacity for longing. Work kept me busy, placid, and, above all, far from San Blas. Life itself was agonizing, and there wasn't a single street that didn't provoke unbearable friction in me, especially the streets of my childhood and teenage years.

I never recovered Eugenia's new boots; I wasn't able to gift them to her. I didn't see her again, the same way I didn't see myself again. Eugenia's world was the world of women, from which I had been banished forever. Thinking about picking up my life from where I'd left it on the stairs leading down to the Bajos de Argüelles stole my breath away. It foretold the next suppressive violence, and I had already had enough. That night, they ripped out my entrails and scattered them on the asphalt to feed trans flesh to the poor rats. I was hollow, beyond fear, subdued. I was a woman, and that couldn't be removed like a tumor, but it could be inhibited if enough pressure was applied. And I did that myself. Applied pressure and locked my cell from the inside.

The thing is, we women are tenacious, and every once in a while, I would scratch at and kick the walls of my cage, screaming and ripping out my hair like a bacchante evicted from the slopes of Mount Kithairon and tossed into a filthy dungeon. That usually ended in the nearest psychiatric emergency ward. I amassed diagnoses of various mental illnesses, and they were never the same. They didn't ask me any questions. They drugged me, they let me rest up for a few hours, and they released me the next day into my brother's care. He was always there to pick up my pieces when I needed him—silent, tender, and frustrated by the distance I put between us, which he didn't know how to navigate. The only thing he could do for me was to return me to my life and wait for the next debacle, like a guardian angel whom fate had dealt a bad hand. I always loved him very much, and I missed him even when he was nearby.

Since there are few forces in the universe more powerful than inertia, mine, which was lunar, led me to try to drink a few more times from what had been my life spring, night after night, but the dragon-men refused to accept my offerings the way they once had. I wasn't presenting myself as I should; I wasn't the same, and I received other liturgies. I discovered that the beauty I'd managed to see in myself in the past wasn't a gift my lovers granted me; it was what I allowed to emerge on those nights. It depended on me, on how I moved, on how I transformed myself into a goddess, and on my exquisite submission. The hands that once accepted a dirty delicacy, the hips that adapted to the rampant femininity I offered them, no longer danced with me the same way. The moment I realized that in that intimacy I was a man like the others, that there was no trace left of me, that they desired me for the wrong reasons, I wanted to disappear, to turn into liquid and slip down a drain, becoming detritus. The spring was dry, and I had to say goodbye to the dragons, my heart broken and my skin cold.

I threw out all my feminine clothes on the second of February 2000, and it was clear that I had gotten rid of more than skirts, dresses, stockings, and shoes. I stood in front of the garbage can until my legs went numb from the cold. I remember the sleet melting on my face and slipping down my recently shaved head. When I couldn't stand the shivering anymore, I left and didn't look back.

I felt humiliated for not having enough grit to commit suicide, unable to reach that state of ultimate bravery that would liberate me from all evil. I felt humiliated by my absolute conviction that years of pain and pure nothingness awaited me before it was all over.

VOLVER

n March 2012, at thirty-four years old, I had to move back to San Blas because I couldn't keep a roof over my head, even with a full-time, steady job. It was devastating. Not so much because of the beating my grown-up pride took or the feeling of failure at finding myself in that situation. I was much more wrecked by the personal aspect than the generational one; seeing the world crumble from capitalist greed and cruelty affected me, but I wasn't alive enough for it to shatter an ego I didn't have. Returning to San Blas was the final nail in my coffin; it completed a circle I never had a chance of escaping, beyond the tortures of a solar being who enjoyed watching me suffer. Every time I had tasted a gulp of fresh air, I'd received an excessive reprisal in return, and what was left of me was just that—subsistence cowed by obedience.

My parents took me in lovingly and seemed thrilled to have me there. They truly were, and I was grateful. They looked at me with tender sadness, and it was as if they'd already discussed it between them and had been expecting me to have to move back in at some point. I was the weak child, the lame dove.

I spent my days out of the apartment. I went into work at ten in the morning; I had a couple of hours for lunch at midday and got off at eight thirty, which always turned into quarter to nine. I would see my parents at breakfast and at dinner. I worked on Saturday mornings too, and usually spent the day and a half I had off in my bedroom, reading or watching movies, running compulsively—sometimes twice a day—to alleviate my anxiety, or taking long walks through Our Lady of Almudena Cemetery. I tried to reciprocate my parents' care and generosity with the same love. But I didn't have much to give. I would break my isolation as often as I could muster the energy, starting with cleaning the bathroom and general scrubbing, which is how you truly show love and respect in a home. I did my best not to skip shared meals and to pay them some attention every once in a while. I'd hidden my entire life from them more than anybody else. It was from them that I'd heard the first words that had convinced me I was deviant, someone who had to hide behind something else, but they loved me fiercely and always knew how to convey that.

It takes a long time to learn that two opposites can coexist, but when you do learn it, you can start unraveling many knots. My mother guarded over me like an old lioness in a time of drought, drawing me closer with her paw, protecting me with her body, her licks taking the form of worried sighs and caresses with both hands on my face, as if propping it up for me. My father was the same as ever: silent, expectant, trying to be the bulwark between me and life, with his elephant king attitude. They weren't that old, but the years of hard work had taken their toll. My father was about to retire; his hair was already completely white, and he moved slowly. He had made a good recovery from his heart issues, but he'd been working since he was ten years old, and a body can take a lot but does have its limits. My mother suffered an advanced stage of a degenerative neurological and bone disease; a medical jury had retired her that very year, but with a pension that was embarrassing for a woman who had never done anything more than bust her hump mopping and scrubbing. She rebelled against her condition with her usual vigor; when the pain let up, she would clean the apartment top to bottom, go out for walks, and did anything she could to squeeze the most out of that comfortable parenthesis.

If only I'd known how to take advantage of those moments of peace, that sanctuary. We'd never had a better situation in which to speak honestly as adults. I could've freed up some of the doubts and guilt that were gnawing away at them, over the first coffee on Sunday mornings—early, while watching life through the windows and thinking slowly but deeply, as if still holding on to that slippery dreamlike quality—or in those silences at the table after meals, when everything's been cleared and washed and there is nothing more to do than let time pass and the sun set. We never had better opportunities to talk. But it wasn't possible. They were convinced they'd made fatal mistakes that had brought me misfortune. I could sense it in their every expression, every gesture, and every reaction to my absent silences. In my chest, in my ribs, in my throat, beat a woman who begged to be able to take the reins. She had the right words; she would have known how, with delicacy and understanding, to take on such a conversation, one that could be rough but promised to be cathartic for everyone.

There was no way to release the pressure. I couldn't see them with adult eyes; I don't know what daughter ever can, or if it's even possible. In their love and protection, I retraced the steps of my life and started stuttering again and conceiving of rejection the way a little girl would. Being trans had forced me to grow up too fast in terms of my self-awareness but had kept me childish and insecure in my closest relationships.

There are families in which love turns into rage and denial as soon as they sense that the ground they are walking on isn't firm. Poorly established loves that respond to a wound with a tourniquet instead of cleaning it well, applying pressure until the bleeding stops, and gently covering it. That was always our case. We loved one another a lot, but we loved one another with too much urgency.

My mother used to sit down and replace missing buttons or finish off some other mending on Saturday afternoons, in those hours before twilight. My father would sit near her, and they'd listen to the radio or turn on the television and ignore it. Meanwhile, in the kitchen, there was always some stew cooking on a low flame for the next day because it was always better after sitting overnight. The whole house smelled of onion, garlic, tomato, pepper, and paprika. Anticipation of the next day's meal was comforting; the smell of food had hope in it. The safety of knowing that, at least for one more day, there would be full plates on the table to gather around, that there would be a tomorrow complete with some hot broth and tender beans.

On some of those afternoons that moved slowly like oil, I dared to take the next step of trying to relate my feelings to them. I started by thanking them for having taken me in, and I asked them how they were doing, if, after the shock of seeing my dire state on arrival, they were now somewhat less concerned. My mother, a lioness in constant alert for her young even though we were old enough to be raising young of our own, cut my words short with that interventionist love of mothers who've seen other mothers bury the bones of their dead babies, fearing the worst.

"You don't need to thank us for anything," she would say, almost angrily. "This is your home; as long as we're alive, you won't want for anything. What you need to do is get better and be okay. You have to be okay. You have to be okay. You have to be okay."

And everything became the echo of her repeating that I had to be okay, when I couldn't even *be*, period. In those moments, my father would get up from the sofa and head to the kitchen to check on the stew, open the fridge, make himself a little open-faced sandwich with whatever he could find, come back to the living room, take a bite, and immediately surrender it to me. It was his way of telling me that he didn't have the slightest idea of how to talk to me, that he had never understood me, but that he was willing to take the food out of his own mouth to nourish me. That he loved me so much, he'd starve for me if need be.

Our family love was always out of sync, and the circumstances hadn't helped us to learn how to communicate. Entire lives spent breaking your back to maintain a home took their toll on everyone.

Fucking work had robbed us of the time and the opportunity to teach one another, and all we had was raw love, which was too powerful. We didn't know how to process it. It made us selfish and demanding with one another; it forced my parents to create impossible expectations for a trans girl. If only I could've been like El Cordobés: brave, a tough guy, a matador, every inch a man.

A DISH OF
MUSHROOMS

eeing Margarita again was like feeling a gust of cold air coil around my spine. An image of a world I'd promised myself was no longer mine, one I couldn't enter without facing unbearable punishment. Margarita was the kind of ghost waiting for me in San Blas, an apparition I didn't need. When you bury yourself alive, you assume everyone else is buried, too; you bring an entire world into the grave with you, a world you thought belonged to you but that, in the end, you formed just an expendable part of.

I was coming home from work one Saturday around three thirty in the afternoon, and there was Margarita in her doorway, extremely thin, with her hair white and unkempt, in a pink housecoat less satiny than the ones she used to wear, and dragging a small oxygen tank, connected to her nostrils, that she removed to smoke. She took a few steps away from the oxygen to light a cigarette and smoked slowly. Seeing her like that, wasted away, I traced inevitable ties to other women in my life. If time had treated Margarita like this, how would Eugenia be, how would that pureblood have confronted the years? In Margarita's deterioration, I saw my own, an inner deterioration; I imagined myself losing my hair, my flesh, my nails, inside increasingly narrower walls.

Again Margarita served as my Pythia, revealing disastrous predictions I didn't want to see. I couldn't face the stab of regret for having abandoned my coven, my other mother, my friend. What kind of bitch does that? The closet had made me selfish; it tore down everything around me to build up its defenses, including lives that weren't my own. Along the way, I abandoned those I no longer needed and those who threatened to shatter so rancorously what I'd constructed. I had come back to the neighborhood out of necessity, and all I wanted was for them to leave me alone behind my battlements of skin, bones, tendons, and dead wood.

"I just saw Margarita; you didn't tell me she was still alive," I said as soon as I entered the apartment, before putting my keys down on the little plate in the entryway.

My mother was browning some slices of garlic to round off lunch.

"Oh, poor thing, she's in terrible shape. She's had cancer for many years; she must be getting near the end."

My mother still kept up the old neighborhood tradition of giving last rites before even saying good morning. The San Blas crows circled around the sick, predicting their deaths so they would have something to talk about.

"She gets her food from the parish; it's really just crap: milk, pasta elbows, tomato sauce, white bread, and chickpeas. Makes me so angry to see that pig of a priest handing out those miserable baskets like he was doing some good. Like the poor don't have the right to anything but bread—it's a damn shame."

"Once in a while, we bring her some tomatoes and cucumbers so she can make a salad," interjected my father. "And your mother saves her a few jars of broth when she makes a big pot. She's in awful shape. The neighbors she had, Señora Reme and La Cosco, they both died. And Asun, Lil Crip, moved to Benidorm to live with a friend. They have a band that sings covers of Las Grecas."

Good for Asun, I thought.

"She's got nobody left in the building. She's all alone!"

"And no pension, of course, or a really low one?" I asked.

"Who's gonna give her a pension, between her years as a hooker and her years getting paid under the table? She probably gets two or three hundred at most."

"Hey, while we're thinking of her, keep your shoes on and

take over some garlic mushrooms. I made enough for an army and already put some aside for your brother. Come on, they're best when they're warm."

My mother was like that; she could be distrustful, but she couldn't stand to see people suffering. She had no idea what she was asking of me, and I didn't have the guts to explain it to her, so I found myself knocking on Margarita's door, one hand holding a hot plate of garlic mushrooms covered with a sheet of aluminum foil and the other sweaty and trembling.

She was slow to answer. I could hear the oxygen tank rolling along the ground, and finally Margarita appeared, peeking through the narrow opening.

"Well, well, darling, what brings you here?" Her chest whistled when she spoke; she was very pale, and her forehead was sweating.

"You recognize me, Señora Margarita?" I didn't know what else to ask.

"Of course, how could I not? You have the exact same face as ever, like a shiny little medallion!"

We both laughed. Of all the descriptions I never expected to hear at thirty-four years old, my face looking like a shiny little medallion was the sweetest and definitely the most unlikely.

"My goodness, how do you come up with these things, señora? A shiny little medallion. Your skin is fabulous, but your eyes must be going."

"Come on in, sweetie, don't stand out there. And, please, don't call me señora. I've known you since you were born."

"I just came to drop off some garlic mushrooms from my mother; they're still warm. I have to get back home. I haven't had lunch yet."

"Sure, angel, thank Jimena for me and let her know I really appreciate it. How are you doing?" she asked as if anticipating my response, scrunching up her face and puckering her lips.

"Okay, Margarita. I'll be on my way. Don't want to keep you."

She didn't insist.

"Come on back for the plate whenever you like and I'll make you a coffee. I'd like to chat and know how things are going for you."

"Sure, Margarita. You take care now."

She closed the door, and I stood in front of it for a while. Mundaneness was destiny's most effective tool, and the first time Margarita and I had had a conversation alone together was orchestrated by some friggin' garlic mushrooms. I sat down on the steps there and figured it was a good moment to reclaim my bad habit of crying alone.

My God, what was I doing to myself, what had I done to myself all these years, what formula of silence had I imposed that could have rotted out my insides like this? Margarita's nearly asphyxiated face kissed me on the cheeks to awaken me like in a poorly told fairy tale. Inside me, a glacier was melting; I could hear the enduring ice crack as it finally surrendered. Nothing had prepared me for that, but all the goddesses who'd been watching over me since I came into this world were expecting it. If only I'd had the guts to stand up and knock on her door and ask her to listen to my confession. I didn't want to go back to that state of newbie tranny in search of a Mother Superior, that world that couldn't be mine, that couldn't be. I again prayed to the elusive God of my milk-and-blood mother to whisk me away from there, even though at the same time, I needed to stay.

The extreme discretion of the new families in San Blas, their tendency to stay inside, worked in my favor. There I was, unable to hold in the convulsive sobs that had been brewing for more than a decade, provoking an echo of gasps throughout the stairwell without anyone approaching me. All because of some goddamn mushrooms and the stupid old neighborhood convention of keeping an eye out for neighbors in need. I took my time recomposing myself and headed back home, thinking of excuses for my puffy red face and why such a simple task had taken me so long.

Another thing I was thinking about was seeing Margarita again. I never was able to give Eugenia her new boots, but I wasn't going to let Margarita be lonely even if it meant having to slap myself awake from dreams again. My defenses had crumbled.

PUSSYCAT IN THE RAIN

bought a French press, four or five packs of coarsely ground coffee, and reminded myself not to forget the milk. Since moving back in with my parents, my meager salary went a lot further; I saved half and still had more than four hundred euros to spend each month. My parents refused to let me chip in or even shop for groceries without asking first. After trying several times, I gave up and understood that, for them, it was nonnegotiable. No matter how old I was, in their house, they took care of putting food on the table, and there was no god in any pantheon that could change that.

I decided that I would use the extra money to ensure Margarita could pick up church baskets less; I'd stock basic groceries so she could stop eating boiled carbs every day. I'd also decided to turn her heat on occasionally and pay her bill; the cold that'd accumulated in the walls was ruining her health almost as fast as the cancer. Nobody should have to live like that.

I got used to going over there some weekday mornings early to have breakfast with her, and on Sundays, I would spend the whole afternoon and evening there, only leaving once I'd gotten her settled into bed with her oxygen tank well positioned beside her. Our relationship developed so naturally that I couldn't stop wondering what would've happened if I'd ever dared to talk to her as a tween. I was tired of what-ifs; I saw every misstep I'd taken in my life as ridiculous and completely avoidable. The violence had been real, and I understood my motivations, but fear had turned the tables on me, and I'd done everything backwards.

Margarita's apartment was jam-packed. It was the fabulously fruity fantasy I'd always imagined, filled with photographs in opulent frames, old but rarely used armchairs with floral upholstery and little lace doilies on the arms. Almost the entire floor was covered with smooth red carpet like in a bingo hall or the staircase of a stage café, and that atmosphere really came to life on one of the living room walls, which was papered in sassy gingham with a gigantic fan imitating a peacock's tail rising majestically up in the center. She had an enormous wooden bed with high posts, made up with a pink fake-satin coverlet.

The first time she gave me the full tour, I wanted to hug her for having confirmed one of my swishiest daydreams. Margarita was my version of Randolph in *Other Voices, Other Rooms*, a character who had branded my life, a transvestite whose house was sinking inexorably into the swamp and only had the strength to raise a glass of bourbon and do her eyelashes. Even Truman Capote would have found it in himself to say a prayer for Margarita if he'd ever met her.

She managed to keep her place clean. She could barely walk a few steps without getting tired, but a little bit at a time, she would run a rag over a piece of furniture one day, a table the next, and on her best days, when she wasn't struggling with the tubes in her nostrils and she had enough oxygen in her blood, she would even sweep a stretch of the floor. The rest stayed clean because it was never used, just gathering dust, which is the breath of time settling on our things so we don't forget it's running out.

"Oh, wow, Margarita, that's some photo." I had been nosing around in a black album with gilded trim she had half-hidden on a shelf behind a horrible ceramic clown figurine.

"Which one?" she asked with a hint of a smile, playing dumb because she knew perfectly well what I was going to find in that album.

"This is too much, Margarita; you look like a young Amanda Lepore. This is too good."

In the photo, she appeared posing, her high heels up as she reclined on a black chaise longue, resting her head on her elbow like a patrician lady awaiting suitors. She was radiant.

"A client of mine named Agustín took that one; we used to have a good time together. That was in a really fun stage café called Lady Pepa, where they would show cheeky little theater pieces. Half of the poofs with money in Madrid went there for drinks. It was run by Mendizábal, the playwright, who was a terrifically amusing nancy and very clever. But further to the right than a cold-water faucet. If I told you all the folks I saw there . . . I'm not one to gossip, but believe me, if I told you, I'd end up dead, just like *La Marilín.*"

She waved me over, and when she figured I was close enough to bypass any bugs planted by the National Intelligence Center, she whispered, "I met Fraga there, and believe me, afterwards I was able to buy two or three pairs of good shoes."

"Fraga?! Are you serious, Margarita? If you're pulling my leg, I'm gonna step on your oxygen cable and leave you dead as a doornail."

"Yes, ma'am. Fraga, Manuel Fraga, the minister, worse than diarrhea with a bad cough and nasty as all get-out."

Imagining Fraga wearing fake eyelashes and licking tranny high heels humanized him a little bit in my eyes; I had to remind myself that he was a bloodthirsty asshole to keep myself from letting him enter the parlor of dignity.

The more time I spent with Margarita, the looser my seams felt. She never asked me anything about my life; she maintained that distance that San Blas had taught us, but she made sure to include me among her equals. She used a feminine "we" as if it were the most natural thing in the world and created a safe space where it was clear I could regroup when I was ready. It gnawed on my conscience to be recovering a space I had already been given. I prayed Eugenia didn't end up hating me; I prayed some saint had revealed to her in dreams what had happened to me.

Margarita's health was quickly deteriorating, but she was happy to have me around. She had less and less mobility and needed more and more help. I committed to going there every night after work to check up on her, make sure she'd had some supper, and help her into bed. My parents didn't question my reasons. I would say they understood in their own way. Perhaps the walls of ice were cracking for all of us. Some mornings, I would find Margarita almost unconscious, without oxygen— she hadn't had time to reach the bathroom and could barely open her eyes. As soon as she regained the tiniest bit of composure, she would smile at me and say, every time, "So nice to have you here, sweetie."

I would quickly wash her body, safeguarding her modesty

and mine. With practice, I got pretty good at it, and we both got used to the idea that it was necessary every once in a while. It was sad, but it was beautiful. I can't think of a more savage intimacy between two women than that sort of two-way dependence where every possible emotional barrier is shattered. She needed me to attend to her body and offer her the dignity her disease was taking from her. I needed her because her company was bringing me back to life.

We decided, with the consent of the doctor who paid her house calls, that she should sleep sitting up in a chair. That would make it easier for her to go to the bathroom and help her breathe better. I would come by her apartment last thing each night, clear up her supper dish, wash her face, apply her lotions, untangle her hair, make sure her housecoat was well closed, and try to wrap her body in a comforter. I would close the door very gently and leave her in the dark, accompanied only by the burbling of the oxygen bubbles and the whistling of her exhausted chest.

The last Sunday we spent together, I dyed her hair the blond shade that had been her signature, the hair I had first known her to have. The dye fumes were no good for her, but at this stage of her illness, it was worth it. Rinsing her hair out was a trial, but I managed with a wash tub, a pitcher, much patience, and a mop. She loved looking into the mirror and recognizing something of the blond Fury she used to be.

During that week, she'd gone from bad to worse. I stayed longer on my nightly visits and came earlier on the morning ones. She spent the day wrapped in a fog that she struggled to emerge from, and she barely ate. I would insist she have a bit of breakfast, then put on her diaper and leave her a bottle of water on a small table beside the armchair she no longer got up out of. All she had to do was extend her arm to reach the water. At night, I would find it almost full. I would bring the bottle to her lips, then clean her up, and I would try to get her to eat something. I didn't force her. If she wasn't hungry, that was up to her.

I tossed and turned in bed, imagining her alone in that dark house. She didn't want to leave any lights on because she said they would lead the Grim Reaper to her.

That weekend, she seemed more active, more clearheaded. I suggested styling her hair, and she found enough energy for that. She had difficulty speaking, having to gather up a lot of air to be able to pronounce the words. It was very tiring, so I would speak, and she would listen with a constant smile. We spent the afternoon with the hairstyling session, and soon the night came with its routines. She ate a little better—some pieces of cut fruit and two cheese wedges, which she loved. When I nestled her into the comforter cocoon, I could tell she wanted to say something, and I drew as close to her as I could to make it easier. She smelled of tuberose perfume and Heno de Pravia.

"Will you leave the record player on?" Her voice was hardly

a voice by that point. Listening to her required interpreting a faint breeze.

I placed the device on a bar cart and rolled it close to her so she could at least turn it off when she wanted to.

"What should I put on, my queen?!"

"'La ... gata ... bajo ... la lluvia.'" "Pussycat in the Rain" by Rocío Dúrcal.

I soon found the album *Confidencias* on the record shelf.

"I'll put on the B side; that's the first song. If you want to hear it again, you just have to lift the needle and place it at the beginning. Can you reach?"

We rehearsed the gesture a couple of times and she managed to do it fairly well. The song began to play, and her eyes grew damp. I drew close again to ask her if she was okay.

"I've ... been ... the ... pussy ... cat ... so ... many ... time ... s. And ... they ... can't ... take ... that ... away ... from ... me."

"I don't doubt it; I'm sure the tigress of Calle Orense was fierce."

I ran a hand over her hair. I kissed her forehead, and we smiled at each other. I left her like that, with a lamp on so she could operate the record player. I left hoping that she would dream of herself that night, the way I had learned to see her in my memories, dressed in white with shiny heels, drunk on life, dancing beneath the rain with all the men who had ever been at her feet.

ALL THE WOMEN

I got up long before sunrise. During that fragment of night, I rested but remained in that state of alertness typically reserved for the night before a trip or an important first day. In that distant consciousness that forces you to feel your way through a wispy darkness as you perceive the passage of time.

It was cold in my parents' apartment, the kind of cold that gets stuck in your chest as soon as you set a foot outside your bed, the kind no heat can thaw. Sweaters, hot drinks, everything feels like a blanket that's too short, that's always leaving some part of your body exposed. I took a long shower, allowing the sponge to linger on each and every part of my body. I tried to do it carefully, as if I cared about my flesh, without my usual rushing and rubbing like a nun in perpetual penitence who had to scrub the devil off her skin. I dressed meticulously; in the top layers of my mind, I wasn't sure why I was doing everything with the slowness of a ritual, although on a deeper level, those thoughts you can't hear in words but can glimpse in the darkness, I did know.

I headed out before the sun had time to break through the horizon's veil. The sky was already changing color, and our street seemed illuminated by an ultraviolet light, like a bruised lip.

I opened the door to Margarita's apartment and saw her seated silhouette, backlit. I could hear the sizzling of the oxygen and the syncopated hum of the record player needle, which had reached the end of the record but obstinately kept reading a surface that had nothing to tell it. I drew close to Margarita to see her face illumined by the little lamp I had left on for her so she could maneuver the record player's arm.

"Good morning, my queen," I said to her body, already cradled by the arms of eternity. "I knew you were going to leave the record on, and that it would keep stubbornly spinning on its axis." My voice was cracking; a gentle, trembling sob was racking my chest. It was so cold. "Let's see if the vinyl is ruined; it's so delicate."

I put the record back in its sleeve and placed it on the shelf between the greatest hits of Boney M. and *La leyenda del tiempo* by Camarón. I moved a lock of hair from her face and tucked it behind one ear. She wasn't cold; she was cool, which is the temperature of surrender, when you no longer have the ability to fight against fever or hypothermia. The absence of defenses, death, is a simple thing of no note; matter changes into a state of mediocrity when the soul shuts down the boiling cauldrons of passion, anguish, love, and anxiety, and abandons the flesh.

I called an ambulance in a soft voice and from another room, as if Margarita could hear me and might get alarmed. I explained the situation in detail twice to different operators, and a team was set into motion and would soon arrive. After that, I called a co-worker to let her know I wasn't coming in that day.

I went back to the living room and pulled a chair over so I could be close to her. I took her hand in mine delicately, the same hand that just hours before had put on "La gata bajo la lluvia" again and again.

"We'll skip breakfast today, my queen. You look pretty. The Reaper's gentle touch suits you. I don't know if leaving the lamp on had anything to do with it; I think she had you on her calendar and didn't need a guiding light." I had to stop frequently to breathe; the heartbreak was accumulating in my throat, and I had to moderate it by expelling air between words.

"Ay, Margarita, it's been lovely but so late. There are so many things I still want to tell you, things you already know, that you probably knew even before I did. You scared me so much when I was a little girl because all my childhood games, all the stories, all the women told me that I was like you. And I didn't want to be like you. I didn't want them to treat me the way you were treated by those cowardly little men, and I insisted on becoming one of them. I was nothing more than a cowardly little man who every once in a while fell in love with the moon, an Endymion who cross-dressed to look handsome, one who let himself be devoured by dragons to shed his flesh and ascend to his mother's right-hand side. I've been my own pimp, my own strict father, and my own jailer, Margarita. And I can't take it anymore. I'm never going to let go of your hand; I'm never going to let go of Mamá Eugenia's hand. I won't let you go completely. You'll be my saints, my moons, my truth-telling mirrors. Can we really be happy, Margarita? If you don't mind, I'm going to keep your black-and-gold album; I need to look at it to remind myself that yes, we have the right to a glorious life, that our hardships are imposed upon us, not something we're born with like a witch's mark. Thanks for everything, my queen. Thank you for the boleros and the stories, thank you for the laughter and the tears, thank you for giving me the kiss of life."

The ambulance arrived; they carried out the obligatory protocol, and I gave them the medical reports and explained the evolution of her illness. They confirmed that her death had been the logical consequence of her disease; the doctor signed the corresponding certificate, and they left. I also made sure to call the municipal undertakers and set up her transportation to the funeral parlor and a proper wake, which I would not attend.

The medical team had carried her to the bed at my request; I wanted her to be comfortable, even in her distance. I lay down beside her and caressed the lapels of her pink housecoat with my fingers. It was stained with food from the previous night, and I couldn't have that. I got up for a soapy sponge to rub out the stain, and when I returned to the room, I could see her complete image like a Marian apparition, like the ascension of a beautiful queen, like a secret the angels whisper into the ears of shepherds. Margarita would leave like the blond Fury she was, like the Empress of Calle Orense. I quickly undressed her, prepared a washtub with water and a few drops of shower gel, dipped a small towel in the soapy water, and washed her body with the same reverence Mary Magdalene would have washed Jesus, with all the care befitting the preparation of a powerful mother to face eternity. Once Margarita was clean, I applied moisturizer everywhere and did her complete facial routine. I chose a long white dress with a halter neck that closed in the back with little crystals; it took me a while to find it amid the tons of clothes she had in her two built-in closets. She insisted on pink, but white was her color.

I applied her makeup very carefully; I was out of practice, but I managed to nail her mature style: "natural but not too natural," as she would say. The marks on her face, the bumps that had embittered my childhood, now seemed like holy ground, and I kissed them slowly. I would honor those dunes of beauty my entire life, and I would see a deity in every woman who bore them, a goddess at whose feet I would toss flowers. No one will ever be as perfect as those transvestites with busted faces. No one ever as beautiful as the women who sacrificed everything to reach a beauty undecipherable to idiot eyes. No woman, nymph, or goddess would ever be as beautiful as the final Margarita I saw disappear beneath the undertakers' white sheet. Before they carried her out of her home, I placed a pair of shoes on the stretcher, white ones with a good heel.

"I'd appreciate it if you'd put those on her for the wake, please."

"Of course, señor," the bearer said to me.

"It's señora," I replied.

He looked me up and down without understanding what I was saying to him, but he corrected himself.

"Okay, señora. We'll tell them to put her shoes on, don't worry."

I sat down on the armchair where Margarita slept, to cry in peace without anxious hiccupping. I cried beautiful, long sobs until I'd purged every last tear.

In the bathroom, I freshened up my face and stared at myself in the mirror, something I hadn't done in more than a decade. To avoid it, I would shave in the shower, underneath the stream of hot water, with my eyes closed, feeling out the limits of my face and its scratchy hair with my fingertips to guide the razor.

The years had been kind to me; it seemed I'd inherited my mother's collagen-blessed skin along with her pretty lips. I didn't have any wrinkles or any other imperfections. It was the moment to prepare the advent of the beautiful queen I had seen when I entered Margarita's bedroom right before decking her out for her final voyage. I pulled out the Velvet Underground's forty-fifth anniversary album and blasted "Femme Fatale."

I went back to her room and undressed like a woman preparing to enter a pyre, eyes forward and defying a fire that only I could see. A hundred ghostly hands supported my legs and back and kept my doubts from weakening my limbs, all the women of the world beheld me: Eugenia, a little bit older, with silver threads in her hair, was smiling in front of a dressing table covered in flowers and looked upwards as if seeking out complicity with an invisible voice; María the Wig waved the branches that were now her arms and greeted my destiny from the tree bark her soul now inhabited; even Jay was swaying on a swing in the moonlight, and he blew me a kiss. I put on a terra-cotta-colored off-the-shoulder dress that fit me perfectly. I did my face with the same makeup I'd used to bid farewell to Margarita. I tousled my hair, which had grown to a vague point between my temples and my jaw. I slipped on some bright red heels, and I went out onto the street where I'd grown up, with my head held high, almost dancing, for the photos at the Figueroa, for Paula,

La Chinchilla, for Daniel and his nine fingers, for Alicia and her skill on the soccer field, for the *grand jetés* that didn't lift Benjamín up to heaven, for the little girl with a patch on one eye who used to dance to songs by Raffaella Carrà and Irene Cara, for the altars on which I had sacrificed myself.

I didn't have a name, but I existed. I inhabited my own legend; I had no name, but I was triumphant Hecuba, Cassandra, Carmilla, Out-in-the-Shed, Snow White's stepmother, La Bikina, La Llorona, the Lady of the Lake, Aphrodite, Cristina Ortiz, Roberta Marrero, Juana Inés de la Cruz, and the May Queen. I was every woman.

A NOTE FROM THE TRANSLATOR

I often say that one of the things I love most about being a translator is that I am always learning new things. I think that's what draws many readers to read as well. Here, Alana S. Portero conveys in fiction a feeling of not belonging that so many of us can relate to, but at the same time she offers us a masterclass in compassion. Like her narrator's left eye, she is telling us to see something. As we follow her, from San Blas—where the void wore a housecoat and lipstick—to the Chueca of the nineties and back again, we realize the fairylike transformation we are rooting for is actually within us, something shifting ever so slightly.

I first grasped that slight shift when I attended the presentation of Alana's book in Barcelona, before it had a chance to become a prize-winning bestseller. In the audience were readers who spoke of devouring the novel, just like you've probably done, but what struck me the most was when Alana talked about the book as an homage to sisterhood—her earnestness as she said that it's something very special, which men truly lack, and that women must remember to never take for granted.

Similarly, as I was checking references within the text, I came across Sylvester. The name didn't really ring a bell, though of course his ubiquitous chart-topping 1978 super hit "You Make Me Feel (Mighty Real)" did. I realized I'd danced to that song, I'd loved that song, and I hadn't understood it. I hadn't known what it was about until I watched the video. In it, I saw Sylvester appear in the half-light, a disco inferno of personality, and I looked into his eyes as he descended those stairs. I saw his tongue moving inside his mouth, enunciating those *l*'s—so strong, so defiant, so real. Sylvester pointed at me, at us, to underscore the word "you" and at the same time dissolve the differences between us. As I let Alana's words move through my fingers, I felt the gift of this communion. Thank you, Alana. Isn't that what we all want? To feel mighty real.